Ac

"I reveled in this collection of tales, in which the novelist/jazz musician Hal Crook delves deftly into a broad spectrum of themes, gifting the reader with not just seven stories, but seven experiences—each one revealing a bit of the author's unique take on human nature, humor and humanity. And you'll never guess who the small brains are in 'Big Brains in Our Midst!' **Jason Camelio, Global Education Professional**

*"*Windborne Tales: Seven Stories *is a must-read collection by novelist Hal Crook. These tales are full of likable and loathsome characters, and packed with delicious jazz references and a native son's take on Rhode Island. In 'Out With a Bang', readers experience the vagaries of life, love, loss and revenge, as though living through them ourselves. Top shelf, well crafted writing."* **Greg Wardson, Pianist/Educator**

Praise for A Brief Madness: New Identity
Hal Crook's debut novel (2019)

"This novel has a lot going for it. Both action and character nuance. The reader wants to know what will happen next, and what will happen to the characters. Agnes is a flawed, multidimensional heroine, whose actions give a moral ambiguity that deepens the novel's message. The jazz references and South Providence as a setting are rich and inviting. Some of Fleck's repartee with other characters is priceless." **Betty J. Cotter, Novelist/Writing Instructor**

"Great characters and story. Female African-American hero is smart and strong. Feels a bit like Walter Mosely. Quality writing with humor and grit." **Robert Nieske, Bassist/Educator**

"Vivid! Intense! I could not put A Brief Madness *down."* **Bill Jones, Saxophonist/Educator**

"A suspenseful story, with interesting characters and at times hilarious dialogue." **Tom Gonnella, Attorney/Guitarist.**

"The author expertly weaves history, intrigue, politics and humor throughout… Impossible to put down." **Julian Shore, Pianist/Educator**

"A truly compelling work of classic crime fiction." **Florian Feuser, Bassist**

"Unpredictable. Unique. Daring. Authentic. And entertaining." **Phil Mazza, Guitarist/Educator**

"It's a whopper of a thriller. I couldn't put it down. And at 95 years of age, I can't wait too much longer for a sequel!" **Peggy Smith, Bookkeeper**

"Terrific debut novel. Certainly in the upper echelon of crime fiction I've read in recent years." **Paul Hoffman, LICSW/Therapist**

"Intriguing story! I didn't want it to end." **David Marr, Master Furniture Builder**

"Characters are multidimensional and well developed…dark and disturbing antagonist, strong and persistent protagonist…balanced with humor and setting." **Mark Esposito, Insurance Executive**

"Expertly crafted first novel…a brutal and unforgiving trip through the changing nature of crime and punishment. A masterful achievement." **MJS**

"A thoughtful, engaging and convincing work of fiction…a genuine page turner." **John Ferrara, Pianist/Author/Educator**

"Fasten your seat belt and get ready for a thrill ride!" **Gene Roma, Percussionist/Educator**

"Intense, thrilling, creative. A masterful first novel." **Jason Camelio, Global Education Professional**

"Great story. I couldn't put it down." **Al Cron, Trombonist/Educator**

"Perfect mixture of humor, compassion, suspense and terror. Kept me turning pages till 3 a.m." **Nancy McDaniel, Artist/Accountant**

"Exciting, well-written novel. Great characters and a roller coaster plot. A wild ride from beginning to end." **Greg Wardson, Pianist/Educator**

"Multidimensional villain and thought-provoking philosophical musings. Well-done first novel." **James Irelan, Guitarist/Poet**

WINDBORNE TALES

SEVEN STORIES

HAL CROOK

Publisher's Information

EBook Bakery Books

Author contact: halcrook1@gmail.com

Author website: www.halcrook.com

Author photo credit: Lucy Cobos

Cover design by Hal Crook

ISBN 978-1-953080-20-2

© 2021 by Hal Crook

Acknowledgments

A literary editor can be priceless. Mine—the novelist, teacher, and writing coach, Jenefer Shute—belongs at the top of that list. I thank goodness every day for her editorial expertise, her words of encouragement and criticism, and her keen sense of knowing what works on the page and what doesn't. Thanks to Jenefer, there's a seasoned professional on the team, cautioning when I stray too far from the path, but respecting my right to. Leaving me enough rope to stretch, but not enough to hang myself. All the while insisting it is my decision whether or not to heed her counsel, which, the wiser and more experienced I become, the more willingly I do. Needless to say, any errors or annoyances found herein—technical or otherwise—are mine alone.

I would also like to express my deep gratitude to the following people for their guidance and inspiration: novelists Rafi Zabor, Betty J. Cotter, and Ron Carlson (for Ron Carlson Writes a Story). And a special thanks to novelist, poet, and publisher I. Michael Grossman, owner of EBook Bakery and devoted big brother to us all, for kindly accepting this manuscript.

Heartfelt thanks goes to the following folks, who have answered the call of friendship with unwavering support and encouragement: Paul Hoffman, Jason Camelio, Dave Marr, John Ferrara, Nancy McDaniel, Greg Wardson, Heinz Czadek, Bob Giustini, Mark Esposito, Ferenc Nemeth, Leo Genovese, Roberto Giaquinto and the usual loving suspects—my wife Joyce and daughter Zoe.

Finally, a story writer's goals are not unlike a jazz player's—about which I have learned a few things over the years: Own your craft as best you can, trust the process of discovery, think with your ears, get out of the way. Create—then curate. Worlds can be formed this way, on the page as well as the bandstand, inhabited by themes and motifs and characters which the hopeful writer (or player) learns about and shapes as they arise and unfold. Welcome to seven such worlds, dear reader, and thank you for investing in this book the most precious commodity of all: Your time.

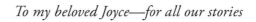

To my beloved Joyce—for all our stories

"Can you do that?" the circus owner asked.
"Sure I can," Millard said. "Just get that lion out of there first."

—Henry Hart
(fictional musician)

"No Billy, I don't listen to prayers. I listen to jazz."

—God
(fictional deity)

Contents

OUT WITH A BANG

It was late afternoon on a hazy early-autumn day, with temps up in the red and humidity that made me wish I was one of Wanda's orchid plants. How she'd keep them with the bromeliads and the ferns in the bathroom or the sunroom, and was always misting them and oh, how they loved it and thrived. The news had gargantuan waves and angry rip currents and fierce unrelenting winds (the reporter's words) pounding the east- and south-facing beaches of Rhode Island, and Hurricane Haroldo stalled a couple hundred miles offshore, threatening a little something extra for the climate change deniers and defenders alike. None of which would have surprised or bemused my wife, Wanda. For whether you believed the weather was changing fundamentally or not—as Wanda used to say—it isn't in the nature of Mother Nature to give a damn what you believe.

I stood alone in the stifling hot waiting area where the air felt like oatmeal, perusing the lost and found notices pinned to a cork board. My nose buried in a hanky to block the odor of disinfectant and animal waste wafting in from the back, where scores of unfortunate creatures deemed non-essential to a world controlled by human desires and priorities had been assigned to coexist. Until their date with Certainty claimed them. Their date with Forever, as my Wanda called it. And as I began ruminating on how we humans so often get it wrong regarding what is essential to our existence and our happiness, a trim woman—holding a long-handled mop and wearing green rubber boots and cutoff jeans and a strapless pink tank top—stepped into the room. The skin on her face and arms and legs and midriff was shiny with sweat. Smooth and taut and shiny. And dark as night.

You're the one who called? she said, huffing and puffing.

I nodded and stuffed my hanky into my shirt pocket. I'm here to adopt, I said, my gaze being diverted from the small raised mole on her cheek by a larger one on her neck.

Species? she said.

Oh, I said, a mutt will do.

A mutt will do, she said, fanning herself with a shiny hand.

Fiftyish, she wasn't just good-looking, but attractive in unusual ways. Like the way her nose did this lunging ski slope kind of thing. And the way the tips of her ears were tapered, elf-like, with an almost translucent quality to them. And the way her short salt-and-pepper hair gripped her head like a bathing cap, exposing the slender nape of her neck. Even the moles added to her appeal.

But it was the way those almond-shaped forest-green eyes rolled over me, slowing here and there for closer inspection, that made me wish (foolishly) that I had appeared as attractive to her.

Well, you're in luck, she said. Seems like we got every last mutt on the planet back there. She smiled and extended a hand. I'm Amy, she said.

Sal, I said, shaking hands. Squeezing harder to parry her grip.

Let's go have a look, she said.

Amy took me behind the counter and down a short hallway into a brightly lit room, with walls of faux-wood paneling painted canary yellow, and a black-and-white checkered linoleum floor covered with rust stains. She chucked her mop into a bucket of sudsy water sitting in the corner, and wiped her face with a towel she'd pulled from behind her belt.

I paused to look around.

The Felines, Amy said. Mommies and kitties over here. Deadbeat daddies over there.

The cages were stacked floor to ceiling and the poor things inside them looked either scared to death or bored to death. I wanted to bring them all home, give them a fighting chance.

Amy watched me take in the spectacle.

What happens to them, I said, if no one—

We don't talk about that, she said. They've got full bellies and a roof. For now. She patted her face and neck again with the towel and walked over to a door at the other end of the room. Pooches are this way, she said.

I followed her into the adjoining space. Noticed another mole, this one on the back of her shiny shoulder. Concrete floor, cement block walls, corrugated tin roof. A few open windows with exhaust fans rattling away. Hanging fluorescent lights with strips of sticky paper dangling from them, laden with flies. A center aisle ran for thirty feet with narrow cages shooting off perpendicular to it on both sides. Each cage held a dog. Or two. Or three.

Amy stepped into the middle of the aisle and held her long thin arms up and open like the Ringmaster at a circus. I give you…the mutts, she said.

There were all shapes and sizes. Some whimpering nervously, some barking incessantly, some curled up in a corner, stone silent. The floor was still wet in the few cages Amy had already tended. A hatched door at the rear of each cage opened to a fenced-in area outside the building where the animals went for air and exercise.

Got no pups today, Amy said, lowering her shiny arms. Last of 'em went yesterday. She looked at me and chuckled. You can use that hanky if you need to, she said. It can get pretty ripe in here. You looking for something in particular?

Oh, anything you've got is fine, I said, breaking eye contact to hide my interest. Mixed breed, if possible, I said. Not too small or too big, if possible. Not too young or too old. Short hair, if possible. Even-tempered, if possible. Healthy…

Amy looked at me. If possible? she said.

I felt a sheepish grin crawl across my face. Well, I said, I'm looking for that gut feeling. You know, the one you get when you know you've found the right one.

Ah, Amy said. The proverbial gut feeling. When you know you've found the right one. She made air quotes with her fingers when she said the words *right one*. Then she walked down the aisle, hips swinging languorously side to side, and stopped at a cage that held a single mid-sized dog.

How 'bout July, then? she said.

The adoption papers said shepherd-lab mix, but you could see spaniel and setter in there, too. In the ears and the coat. After we finished with the formalities I made a donation to the shelter. A good-sized one, hoping to impress. Create a memory. Amy handed me the leash and the three of us walked out to my car.

The wind had died down and the temperature had plummeted and the humidity was abating. Par for southern New England, I thought. Amy's skin was still as smooth and taut as before, just not as shiny.

I love animals, I said.

Gotta love an animal lover, Amy said, winking and presenting me with her card. *Creature Comforts Animal Shelter*, it said. *Amy Dunn, Innkeeper.* At the bottom was a website and an email address and the days and hours of operation. I turned it over and saw a handwritten phone number on the back. Small and neat, like print.

My mobile, Amy said, eyeing the card. In case you have questions. Or need help. She folded her arms across her chest and turned her emerald gaze on me. With July, I mean.

I took the card and pocketed it with the hanky and extended my hand.

Amy slipped hers into mine. No firm grip this time, just a gentle grasp. Like holding hands, almost. It was nice to see our hands entwined, I thought. Her black one and my white. After a moment, we let go.

Looks like we've been spared, Amy said, gazing up at the sky.

She changed directions on us, I said.

She? Amy said.

Mother Nature, I said.

Well, she said, the reports did say a change of direction was unlikely. But possible.

Change, I said. It's always hard. Even for hurricanes.

But possible, Amy said, her eyes open wide, the vibrant leafy green drawing me in.

Yes, I said. This time.

And then I realized something; it was like a switch had been thrown. This was the first time it felt okay—good, actually—not to be wearing my wedding ring.

Keep me posted, Sal, Amy said. She's a love. We'll miss her around here.

Oh, I said, we'll visit. Often, I said.

We got home around supper time. The leaves on the giant elm in the front yard were already starting to turn. Soon there would be colors on those branches that every artist would dream of finding on her brush someday. Flaming reds, burnt oranges. Flaxen yellows, tawny browns. I've always loved this time of year—except for the hurricanes and the gargantuan waves and angry rip currents and unrelenting winds—when the tourists would be gone and Wanda and I would take our vacation up north. Visit a mountain, stay in a tent or rent a cabin. Skinny dip in the lake and make love in the canoe, or in a field of tall golden grass. Or not so tall. Sometimes we'd go with our friends Blake and Sheila, up until Sheila, and then Wanda, passed. And it all came to an end.

I pulled up the gravel drive and got out and went to the other side of the car and opened the door. July was waiting for me in the passenger seat, those big droopy eyes melting me.

C'mon girl, I said, in an excited whisper. That old storm missed us, I said. Changed course on us. Luck was with us, girl. This time.

She caught the vibe in my voice and hopped right out. Long bushy tail wagging like a wind-up toy. Happy to be anywhere but inside that cage back at the shelter.

Bet you miss Amy, I said to her. Shiny Amy, I said. So do I, I said. Don't worry, girl, we'll visit soon.

She limped up the weed-happy brick walk to the tiny lime-green cape Wanda and I had lived in for the thirty-five years we were married. Up until Wanda succumbed. Almost two years ago it was, a few months after Sheila. It got Wanda in her ovaries, Sheila in her breasts, and then her lungs. No kids, Wanda and me. We quit after our first and only perished on her second birthday. Cecily, her name was. After Wanda's mother. She'd have been twenty-one this year.

I looked up at the house and tried to imagine what July must be thinking. The place had needed work for some time. Paint, roof, siding, doors, windows, gutters. The yard was a sight too, all wild and overgrown. The fence looking like a toothless smirk, missing more pickets than not. I'm sure a hurricane would not have helped any, but it couldn't have made things much worse. The neighbors tried not to be upset about the way I'd let things go, starting back when Wanda first got sick. They said they understood the situation and could sympathize. But there were limits.

July seemed fine with everything.

When we got to the front door I knelt down and patted her on the back and rubbed her behind the ears. All floppy and hairy. She licked my hand and pushed her cold wet nose up under my arm.

Welcome home, July, I whispered. Who's a good girl? I said. Are you a good girl? Yes, you are.

She let out one of those happy Lassie-style barks. Woof! *Great to be with you, Sal.* Woof! Woof!

Best friends already.

Amy had named her July because that's when she showed up at the shelter. On the Fourth of July. Probably abandoned, Amy said, since no one had called or come by to claim her. A trucker had dropped her off and left a note after nicking her while she was crossing the highway. She was lucky, Amy said. The vets were able to save her legs.

They estimated her age at around seven or eight based on the condition of her teeth and eyes and coat. Her attitude and pep. But seven or eight in dog years means between fifty and sixty in human years, so I decided not to give her a new name. Why try and teach an old dog new tricks, I figured. Why introduce change at this point, pressure her to learn things all over again, things she already knew. I could relate, being an old dog myself and not at all fond of change. Not my thing, change. Everything about it being so…different.

But some things can't be helped. Or changed. Change being one of them.

When I mentioned to Amy—before we left the shelter—that I wouldn't be changing July's name, and the reason why, she said Aw in this warm melty voice that made the hair on my arms stand up. And there's no forgetting the look she gave me.

That's so sweet of you, Sal, Amy said. You and July.

A few months after Wanda's funeral, my friend Blake had recommended meds and psychotherapy, neither of which had worked for him when the disease took Sheila, but he thought they might for me. Blake didn't buy into the whole therapy thing for himself. He'd shake his head and say funny things like, *Anyone who goes to a psychiatrist should have his head examined.* Then he'd say, But who knows, Sal? You might be the exception.

At first I didn't take my situation seriously. But after waking up down in the dumps every day, I realized I was stuck in some kind of doldrums, and needed help. So I went on line and found a licensed social worker who called himself a small-time therapist, and figured that was better than someone who called himself a big-time therapist, and signed up. Acute depression caused by the loss of a life partner and the end of a career, is how he put it. *Feeling bad for good reasons*—is how Blake put it. It all made sense to me.

So for the past two years there's been enough small-time therapy to cure a religious cult, and enough Paxil to ignore all the unwanted thoughts you could ever want, and enough social media to numb everything else that might be bothering you, including social media. Blake enjoys the phenomenon of social media, since he's much more the sociable type than me. He likes meeting people and hearing their stories and telling them his. Maybe it comes from being a musician, a professional jazz musician in Blake's case. But he also makes these interesting art structures by welding things together. *Blake Blakey—Jazzman/Welder* it says on his card.

The shame of it is, Blake has taken Sheila's death harder than he lets on. Keeps it all inside. Won't get help, won't accept it. Knows he needs it. I believe the loss has changed him. Damaged him, actually, like loss can do. Sometimes I think I should be more concerned about how things have changed for both of us, how the damage has made reality a lot more... real. How it has deepened our awareness—if not our acceptance—of the main fact of life: that we can live decent lives and fight the good fight every day, but in the end we still lose everything. Sometimes instantly. Sometimes gradually—and then instantly. I think it has brought us closer to the edge, Blake and me. I think we teeter on it at times. And if there's one way that we are alike now—a way that neither of us would ever have guessed—it's that, in the face of such powerlessness, we both like the idea of going out kicking and screaming. With a bang. Getting even any way we can. Eye-for-an-eye style.

After Sheila passed, Blake came over and fixed the leaks in the vintage tin soaking tub I inherited from my grandparents, and then he installed it in the bedroom for us, to help with Wanda's joint pain from the chemo. He said Sheila could soak all day long in the tub. And did Wanda ever love those baths, too, with me soaking in there with her. Right up till the end, when she'd finally had enough. Enough of baths. Of plants. Of me. Of everything.

God, how I miss…everything.

But this Internet deal is wasted on me. I don't care about technology or politics or people in the news. Celebrities. The famous-for-being-famous types. I'm not curious about what they eat or drink or think or say. I don't need to see pictures of them in their homes, or their fancy cars. Their fancy bathing suits, or their pajamas. I couldn't care less about the digital age, the fancy new ways of doing things. I'm not like Blake in that way; the old ways are fine for me. Blake and Mother Nature can go be their mercurial selves and change it up all they want. I'm happy with things the way they are. Or were.

Well, not *happy* happy. But. You know.

And you can say whatever you want about pets, but they do bring you a certain kind of…certainty. And the happiness that comes with it. If you haven't experienced it first hand you might not understand how you can wind up preferring a pet to the people in your life. To people period.

That's what happened to July and me. We started out as friends and in no time became family. Team July, Amy dubbed us one day while we were visiting. It was at the end of our second month together—July, Amy and me. It's all still fresh in my mind, the events of that day. Raw, I think, says it better.

I was getting ready to retire after thirty years as a race-relations counselor at Rhode Island Community College, and had started making plans for the good life. Things had been looking up since Amy and I had started dating. Movies, museums, dinners, quiet nights on the couch, reading. There was companionship and mutual appreciation. Common interests. No sex yet, but you didn't need binoculars to see it on the horizon. Amy had mentioned that our hello and goodbye hugs and kisses were lasting longer, and getting more intimate. Which gave us both a chuckle. And then one night, while I was sitting on the couch with my arm around her shoulders, she laid her arm down along my leg and turned a page in her book. Then she left her arm there and continued reading. The promise of things to come, I thought. I looked into those magical eyes. Don't you just love love? I said. Amy nodded. Gotta love a love lover, she said.

So there was excitement in the air; I could feel it and July could, too. Dogs can feel certain things even better than humans. Smell them, even.

Like the pheromones we give off when we're excited, or nervous, or afraid. And she must have sensed or smelled someone in the house who wasn't supposed to be there when we got home from visiting Amy at the shelter that day. The day Amy had dubbed us Team July.

Now, July was no attack dog. Not even close. Love at first sight being her default setting. But as soon as we got inside the house she started making this low steady growl deep in her throat. I'd never heard a sound like that come out of her before. I whispered to her, Come on, girl, and we started walking through the house. Every now and then with July making that quiet growl, so soft and low you had to be listening or you'd miss it.

When we got to the bedroom she suddenly stepped in front of me and blocked my passage. A voice in my head said to leave right then, but we didn't. She peered into the room through the open door, head cocked, ears scissoring. She looked back at me, then at the room. At me, at the room. And then came that growl. It seemed like she was trying to warn me about something, but didn't want to warn the something about me.

I wish now that I'd listened to that voice in my head, and that I didn't get such a good look at him before he knocked me down. The raised scar cutting diagonally across his right eyelid and running down his cheek, the long curved Arabian dagger tattooed on his forearm. And then, when he hit me again with that wooden club, that did it for July, and she went for him. Locked her teeth onto the arm that held the club, and would not let go.

He punched her and he kicked her and he screamed at her, and she growled and clamped down all the harder and just took the beating he was giving her. At one point she shook her head and ripped open his arm and tore into the flesh. There was blood everywhere, and the next thing I knew, he'd switched the club to his other hand, and then came a hard thud and a muted yelp. He stood hitting her until finally her jaws opened and she fell limp on the floor.

I crawled over to her and took her into my arms, and when I looked up through my tears, he was gone. As was Wanda's jewelry, the necklaces and earrings and bracelets I'd given her over the years. Her wedding ring. All of it, gone.

July, too.

I still see him every day in my mind. And in my dreams at night. Those angry eyes glazed over in shock. The scarred eyelid and tattooed arm. The blood on the wall and the floor. His. Mine. July's. I still hear the thud of that club and her muted yelp, July going out with a bang. Kicking and screaming. Quietly. And worst of all, that voice in my head telling me to get out of there. And I didn't.

I wish I didn't see it all and hear it all so clearly. The violence. The violence is the hardest thing to forget. And to stomach. Whether it's from a wooden club, or some hideous disease like Wanda's, or Cecily's accident, or just plain old age, the snuffing out of life is a violent act. It's just a question of degree. Ask me, there's no such thing as non-violent death. Even when it's the so-called peaceful kind. It's the violence that cuts deep, and does the real damage.

But some things can't be helped. Or changed. Sights and sounds and past decisions being some of them. It's crazy to say, I know, but if only we could choose what could be changed and what couldn't, it wouldn't be so hard.

Amy agreed. Blake did, too. Some things just can't be helped, Sal, they both said.

Four weeks later, on my 65th birthday—a bright and beautiful Wednesday it was—I was sitting at my desk in the den, surfing the web and thinking what a boredom-breeding sickness this social media business is. Who could've thought it up? Who put the ME in media? Had to be some deranged person, I decided. Having become one myself, I was just glad it wasn't me. A knock came on the door and I got up and walked to the living room and looked out the window and saw Blake on the landing, looking more scruffy and unkempt than ever. It had been several days since I'd seen him last, and change you don't keep an eye on can sneak up and happen fast to us older folks.

I opened the door. Blake, I said. What's up? You're looking all…disheveled. Everything okay?

It's time, Sal, he said, wild-eyed.

Time? I said. For what? A shave? A bath? Some clean clothes?

You know what, he said. We have a date. Today.

A date? I said.

Come on, he said. He turned too quickly and stumbled down the landing. Then he righted himself and headed for the car.

God, this place is a mess, he said, scanning the property. You need to spruce it up, Sal. The neighbors.

We got inside Blake's Fusion, now missing both sideview mirrors and smelling of body odor and something more…tangy. Urine, maybe.

Time for what? I said, again. Blake didn't answer. He started the car and pulled away.

What's this all about, Blake? I said, thinking it might be my birthday. He looked out the window and pressed down on the gas, smiling in a strange way I had not seen him smile before.

We rocketed down Route 1 heading south, out past the hospital and the residential area where we lived and into a less populated rural area.

Blake, I said, watch out for cops. They hide all along this stretch of highway, I said. In the blind spots after the bends in the road.

Half an hour later we approached the town of Wilderville, Rhode Island, sitting several miles in from the coast on the border with Connecticut. The dense woods and thick oak tree canopy that had made 1A feel like a tunnel thinned abruptly to reveal not a Walgreens or a CVS, but a Wilderville Pharmaceuticals; not a Home Depot or even a Benny's, but a Harvey's Hardware & Surplus; not a McDonalds or a Burger King, but a Berger's Burgers. And how did a beauty salon—my Wanda would've wondered—get plopped on top of the post office, itself the size of our one-car garage.

Look there, Blake, I said, pointing to a street sign that read: Dirt Road.

Blake hadn't said a word the whole time. Driving through town at a crawl, he kept looking out the window and watching with that distant look in his eyes. I sensed it was a serious matter, whatever it was we were here to do. At one point I felt the skin grow tight across my face as it occurred to me what that might be.

We pulled to the curb in front of a diner set some distance off the road. Mounted on a post was a blue neon sign. Fanny's Fast Food, it said. A big picture window gave the patrons inside a view of the street. Blake shifted into park and let the engine idle and then he rolled down his window. I rolled down mine and my head filled with the smell of cooking grease from the ventilation fans on the roof of the building. It was around noontime and I was feeling hungry.

Blake, I said, are you feeling hungry?

Blake sat watching a couple of teenage boys shooting hoops at a public court in the little tree-lined park across the street. One of the boys was tall and skinny and black, and the other was short and chubby and white, with red hair. Good, I thought, let the races mix and hang out together, work and play in harmony. Be good for everyone if we could recognize ourselves in each other. These boys were playing hard and scoring. Blake gave a curt nod of his head each time one of them sunk a basket.

But they weren't the only ones. Two women with baby carriages sat on a bench in the shade at the end of the court. One of them threw her head back and laughed at something the other one said.

It's in the glovebox, Blake said, still watching the boys play.

What is? I said.

There, he said, pointing, but not looking.

I pressed the latch on the glovebox door and it dropped open. I rummaged through the loose papers until I felt it. I looked at Blake, still watching the court.

I took it out and held it in my hand. It was smaller than I had imagined, and heavier than it looked. A dull charcoal gray a few shades darker than Blake's Fusion—a hue you would not be seeing on the leaves of turning trees. I laid my hand in my lap and felt the weight of it on my leg. The cold hard heaviness of it. It felt good, that heaviness. Not good like Amy's arm had felt, but better than Paxil, and therapy, and Facebook ever did.

I closed the glovebox door. Blake was watching the park, the boys playing and scoring, the women rocking their baby carriages with their free hands. I turned the gun barrel toward myself and looked into the small circular chambers. There were six of them, but only one held a bullet.

It only takes one, Blake said. One's enough if you're feeling lucky. He looked at me. Unless you're feeling extra lucky, he said, and handed me two more rounds.

I pocketed the extra bullets and then I realized that Blake had been right about me knowing what it was time for. Deep down I had known what this date was all about all along. *Out with a bang*, as we had discussed.

I opened the car door and got out and walked across the street and stood some twenty feet behind the women and felt the skin grow tight across my face again. I didn't expect to do this. Blake hadn't expected me to do it, either. He yelled my name. Sal! The women turned to see what was up and I gave the barrel a spin. I wasn't thinking about the women, or about what I was doing out there, only about the beginning of the end of something.

The women saw the gun and screamed. They jumped up and started to run, pushing their carriages in front of them, shielding them with their bodies. The boys had stopped playing and were standing still and watching, the black one holding a phone to his ear. The white one said something and they both turned and ran. I stood there in a daze. Things were happening so fast, but in slow motion, too, like in a dream. I walked back to the car and opened the door.

Blake leaned over the seat. Get in, Sal! he said.

I got in. Police sirens were wailing in the distance. Blake pointed to some people standing in the window of the diner, looking out at us. I glanced at them as I reached to close the door. Blake rolled up his window and we sped off like daredevils, the tires screeching and leaving burn marks on the pavement.

A feeling came over me at that moment. I knew this feeling, but hadn't felt it in ages, probably not since childhood. I'd call it Certainty. With a capital "C". And the happiness that comes with it. I told Blake about the feeling and he said that he understood. That he had felt it too, and had made up his mind about it a long time ago. Soon after Sheila had died.

We drove the rest of the way home in silence. When we got there Blake pulled up the drive and let me out. I walked around to the driver's side.

This place is a mess, Sal, he said. You need to spruce it up. The neighbors.

I looked at him. You're telling me to spruce it up? I said.

He dismissed my comment with a wave of his hand. Then he said, Keep it. It's yours.

Thank you, Blake, I said. I will.

Did you see him? Blake said. In the window? At the diner?

I eyed Blake coolly. How did you know? I said.

That's where he works, Blake said. I was in there one night, at the counter. Heard him talking to some folks down the other end. He was showing them his arm, like it was some kind of trophy. All scarred up. Dog bite, I heard him say. Said he had to beat the thing dead before it let go. Bragged about how he made out with the jewelry.

I flinched when I heard the word dead, and again with jewelry.

When I went to pay my bill, Blake said, the bastard surprised me. Said no charge for the homeless. I told him I got a home, and the S.O.B. looks me over. Says, I'm talkin' one with floors, and walls, and a roof.

Blake shook his head.

Well, I said. Did you pay him?

Blake's brows grew together. And ruin the sting? he said. No way. I might be ninety percent pecans, and the rest of it polyester, but I'm no fool, Sal. Free pie and coffee means free pie and coffee.

Permanent pressed polyester, I said.

He smiled. Happy birthday, Sal, he said.

I stepped aside and Blake backed out. I watched him drive away and then I went inside to the kitchen and sat down at the table.

I took the gun from my pocket—still loaded with the single round—and gave the barrel a spin. Out with a bang, I thought. I put the muzzle to my head and felt the skin grow tight across my face. My heart started to race and I thought about the beginning of the end of something. I thought about the feeling that had come over me while speeding away from the diner in Blake's car. The feeling of Certainty, with a capital "C". And the happiness that comes with it. How rarified a feeling it is. How glorified. How desirable.

How imaginary.

Then I pulled the trigger and heard the dry metallic click of the hammer slam into an empty chamber, and I thought, Empty. Like my life had been since Wanda had been taken. July. My career. Cecily. My sanity. To have had them all, and lost them all... I wondered why there was no natural justice, why justice wasn't automatic. Why fairness—a simple eye for an eye—had to be fought for. Won. I thought about Amy. About our few promising months together being yet another beginning of the end of something, like everything else. About beginnings always leading to endings, and how you can never change that. About not wanting to feel that anymore.

I thought about how I'd missed my date with Certainty just now. With Forever, as Wanda had put it.

And then something moved inside me, slightly, but enough so that I felt cut off. Cut loose. And I knew what it was I must do.

Blake's gone now. It was on his ninth try when his luck finally ran out and Certainty claimed him. His ninth date with Forever. No world record there, but a darn good run. Sitting in the Fusion parked by the curb at Fanny's Fast Food. There was no dry metallic click of the hammer slamming into an empty chamber this time. No one shooting hoops and scoring. No one in the park pushing baby carriages. No one watching from the diner. Just...*Out with a bang.*

It was in all the papers. Blake had been a colorful person around town. A traditional-style jazz trumpet player of some renown, trying to reinvent himself as a modern free-jazz player and losing all his gigs in the process. Classic Blake. He used to say things like, Playing free jazz is nearly impossible to do well, Sal. There is no greater challenge to an improviser's musicianship, he'd say, than to try and create a sense of musical form within the formless. It's like playing free chess, he'd say. Imagine trying to make sense of the game without any rules, Sal? How would you know you've won? Or lost? You have to forget the rules without forgetting about them, he'd say, and do that after spending your whole life studying and learning them. It's like playing God, in a way, Sal. You have to be crazy to even try.

I give him credit for that. Being crazy enough to try.

The police came and talked to me about it after they searched his place and found a photo of us—Blake and Sheila and Wanda and me—on vacation up north in the mountains. Blake had written the date and our names—Sal and Wanda Withers—on the back of the photo, which is how the police knew to contact me. We sat in the parlor—me in my Stickley armchair, the cops on the Biedermeier by the window—while I told them about Sheila, and about Wanda. They asked if I was feeling all right and what did I intend to do now. In other words, was I crazy enough to try and follow in Blake's footsteps.

The question took me by surprise, and I asked them whatever gave them that idea. They said there was this fellow who worked at Fanny's Fast Food, who had identified me in the picture as the one in the park who had showed off a gun back when Blake and I had first visited. I told them it wasn't me and that that fellow was mistaken, I'd never do anything like that.

I told them how Blake enjoyed meeting people and hearing their stories and telling them his. How he embraced the phenomena of social media and the digital age and liked doing things in fancy new ways, his music and his welding. And that it even cost him all his gigs but still he didn't care. I told them that I'm different than Blake. That the old ways are fine with me. That climate change and probably every other kind of change is headed down the pike straight at us, and there's nothing anyone can do about it. So we'd better just try and be ready. I told them I'm living the good life now, and whoever that guy was in Fanny's Fast Food, he must've been seeing things.

They sat there listening and not saying anything. And then, when I'd finished, they said, Okay. And got up and left.

When I told Amy about Blake she came right over and said she was worried about me. Blake and I were close, she said, and had experienced similar trauma. We talked about that, and as we did, one thing led to another, and we ended up somewhere I would not have expected. In bed. Together. Finally.

Afterwards—with our bodies still entwined, her black one and my white, her skin smooth and shiny and dark as night, her emerald eyes aflame—Amy asked me to come with her on the two-week trip to Washington D.C. she had been planning, with the intention of visiting family and seeing our nation's Capitol. Under the circumstances (and now the covers), she said she did not want to leave me here, alone.

I promised her I'd be okay, that I wasn't like Blake, and that as long as she was planning to come back there was nothing to worry about. Which I hated to do, lie to her like that. But with Amy gone, I knew it would make things easier.

The day before she left, she called and said a new mutt had arrived at the shelter.

She's a rescue, Sal. So adorable. Her name is Francis.

Francis? I said. How'd she get a name like Francis?

Well, if you saw her you'd understand, Amy said. She looks just like a Francis. So I had to name her—

Well, I don't want to see her, Amy.

But Sal, one look and it'll be over. You won't be able to resist. I'm talking gut feeling. When you know you've found the right one.

Sorry, I said.

But she's so full of life, Sal. She'll outlast us both.

Can't do it, I said.

Mixed breed, Amy said. Not too young, or too old. Not too small, or too big. Short hair. Even-tempered. Healthy...

Thank you, Amy, I said. But I've had my fill for this go-round.

Amy has called three times a day for the past seven days from Washington. To check on me. Doesn't hide her concern. I've tried to reassure her, but she says she can't help it, she's afraid for me. For us.

How does she know, I wonder?

But it doesn't change anything. Because, as we know, some things can't be helped. Or changed.

Clive Detesto finished his shift at eleven. It was dark in the parking lot behind Fanny's Fast Food where I sat waiting for him in the back seat of his battered Mercury Marquis, like the assassins do in the movies. But in this case, ankle deep in empty beer cans and burger wrappers. Beats me what a crucifix was doing mounted on the dash. Based on my snooping, this was a guy who wouldn't be missed at his own funeral.

Clive showed up around 11:15, and I thought he might try and run away or yell something after he got in behind the wheel—still wearing his apron and smelling of cooking oil—and felt the gun at the back of his neck. But he didn't. He kept his eyes glued on me in that rearview mirror and did exactly as I told him. I could see the beads of sweat forming on his skin, and by the time we pulled up the drive to my little run-down place, his shirt collar was soaked.

I held the gun on him and made him put his hands behind his back and cuff himself like Blake had explained, and then I took him inside and sat him down in the kitchen and gave him a soft drink laced with downers, which I held for him while he drank through a straw.

After he passed out, I dragged him to the bedroom and dropped him into Wanda's soaking tub, and then ran the cuffs behind the metal bar Blake had welded to the bottom of the tub basin for me. I cuffed Clive's arms behind him just above the elbows, so his head couldn't reach more than halfway up, and then I stoppered the drain and turned on the water and let it run. Clive Detesto wasn't going anywhere. And with Amy out of town for another week, it would be just the two of us.

When he came to, I stood before him. That cut-loose sensation coursing through me like horses on fire.

How's the arm, Clive? I said.

He thrashed about the tub, eyeing me.

Your goddamn dog ruined it! he said. How'd you find me?

Oh, I said, some homeless guy tipped me off. Customer of yours.

He squinted at me, and then it dawned. Son of a bitch, he said. From the diner!

A ruined arm, I said, for a ruined life. That seem fair to you?

Fair? he said, the panic building. Fair? What the hell is fair?

I held up the gun and emptied all the bullets Blake had given me into my hand and re-loaded a single round. I waited till the water had reached Clive's ears and he was about to go under and then I gave the barrel a spin and held the gun to my head and felt the skin grow tight across my face. *Horses on fire.* I looked down at Clive and saw the horror enter his eyes as he realized that should I be unlucky…

I don't suppose you still have the wedding band, I said. Cheap little gold-plated thing? Wanda wore it every day, I said. For thirty-five years.

Clive was straining to keep his head above the water.

I didn't think so, I said.

I counted down from five and pulled the trigger.

The hammer slammed into an empty chamber and the panic in Clive's face subsided. I stepped closer and held the gun between his eyes. Out with a bang, I said. A ruined life for a ruined life. Eye-for-an-eye style.

I counted down from five again.

Clive screamed, his voice a bubbly, watery shriek.

I pulled the trigger.

Again the hammer slammed into an empty chamber.

The water was up to his nose and he was choking on it.

Nice work, Clive, I said. We delayed our date with Certainty. With Forever, as my Wanda called it. Luck was with us, Clive, I said. This time.

Clive was trying to kick the water out of the tub.

I reached and turned off the tap, imagining what must be going through his mind. How surprised he must have been that it wasn't a bullet. How much regret he must be feeling now for what he'd done.

I left Clive there to soak it all in, and went to my desk and took out a pen and paper. I wrote:

> Dear Amy,
>
> It has been one of the greatest pleasures of my life to spend time with you. And such quality time it has been. But more than pleasure, it has brought me a good measure of happiness. You and July appeared at my lowest point and raised it to a height I would not have thought possible. To Team July! Thank you. And now I must do something that will probably disappoint you when you find out, and so I want to apologize while I can.
>
> Faithfully, your animal lover,
> Sal

It was five days ago that I wrote my letter to Amy. I put it on her kitchen table this morning so she'll have it when she gets home, since I'm having serious doubts at this point. Because if you could have observed the goings-on at my place today, on this bright and beautiful Wednesday, you would have seen me standing by the tub in the bedroom, eyeing a swarm of dust motes swooping weightlessly in the sunlight that streamed in through the window; and you would have noticed the calendar on the wall reading September—when today is actually April 30th—with a picture of a lonesome stretch of rocky coastline and a field of tall golden grass bending slantways in the wind, conjuring up melancholy thoughts about the beginning of the end of something.

And you would have seen the Smith & Wesson in my hand, as I slung the empty barrel open and loaded *two* rounds into adjacent chambers, and then closed the barrel and gave it a spin and released the safety. And when I brought the muzzle to my head and gazed down at the man in the tub—the water at his shoulders and climbing toward his ears—it would have occurred to you, as it certainly did to him, what I was about to do.

And when I pulled the trigger and you heard the dry metallic click of the hammer slamming into an empty chamber—and then saw me do it to the man in the tub, and again heard the dry click of the hammer—you would never have guessed that it was the fifth time this had happened in as many days, and therefore you would not have thought, What were the chances of that happening—with two chambered rounds!

And you would not have wondered how such a ritual could be what made someone feel like his life was worth living, just to see how long he could postpone his date with Certainty. With Forever. Eye-for-an-eye style. Where his beloved Wanda, and his Cecily, and Blake and Sheila, and July, would be waiting for him.

And if you kept on watching, you would have seen Amy racing up the driveway just now. Jumping out of her car and running to the house, chased by what in all likelihood was a rescued mutt named Francis. Yet another beginning of the end of something, you would have thought.

Change does sneak up and happen fast to older folks, you would have thought. Whether you keep an eye on it or not.

Sal! you would have heard Amy cry. Open the door.

Oh Certainty, you would have heard me say. And the happiness that comes with it.

Sal, let me in! I'll use my key if you don't open the door.

How rarified a feeling it is.

I'm inside, Sal. I have Francis.

How glorified.

Team Francis, Sal.

How desirable.

We're here for you.

How imaginary.

Sal, don't!

Woof!

ALL THAT COMES OUR WAY

Like most people, I received my names at birth. In my case, the patronymic surname Seeks (an altered spelling of Seeck, of German origin, from a short form of a compound name formed with sigi, meaning victory); and the toponymic given name Clifford (of English origin, meaning ford by a cliff). Nothing in the middle, in my case. But all the kids in my neighborhood—except for one, and she's gone now—call me Whacks. An epithet I am not at all pleased about. Which came from the arguably deranged mind of my occasional best friend, Ziggy Zigarelli (an altered spelling of Zegarelli, of Sicilian origin, a metonymic surname meaning maker of ribbons), whose given name is Zosimo (of Greek origin, meaning full of life). And who has a knack for coming up with offensive but in some way relevant nicknames that stick.

Ziggy and I were born on the same day (April 2) and in the same year (1948), with me arriving half an hour before he did. And there is a lifetime of wisdom in those thirty minutes.

We had our fourteenth birthdays last month, and so you might find it odd that I have written this story—a memoir, of sorts—the first of many to come, I predict. You'll likely recognize the general storyline, but I'm fairly certain none of the characters will ring a bell. A significant one being my mother, orphaned at three and raised in foster homes until she went off to college. A kind and uber-intelligent woman, who dislikes confrontation and warns about having expectations, and tends not to stick up for herself when it's called for. An attractive and resourceful woman as well, who has weathered more than her fair share of adversity and heartbreak in life. If not always with a smile, then with courage and grace and…well, resourcefulness.

Another major—albeit loathsome—character is her current husband, my unofficial stepfather. An unlikely suitor who won her favor with sweet talk and cajolery, and, of all things, dancing (she loves to dance, Ballroom style). A professional drinker with a two-plus-pack-a-day smoking habit, and all the broken capillaries and bad breath and nicotine-stained teeth and fingers to prove it. A troubled man, who once joined the United States Marine Corps and shortly thereafter was informed that his services as a soldier would no longer be required, sparing him a horrific and potentially lethal landing on the beaches of Normandy and securing a stressful future existence for my mother and myself. (Knowing him as I now do, I'd have to say the Marines got it right, since I cannot see him as the type to give a fig about fighting our country's battles, in the air, on land, and sea, from the Halls of Montezuma, to the shores of Tripoli.) And, most recently, a man who lost the sight in one of his eyes through no fault of my mother's or my own. Although he would say he sees it differently. (His pun.)

Since before I was born, my mother, Roberta Olsen Seeks (Olsen, a patronymic surname of Danish-Norwegian origin, meaning son of Ole; given name Roberta, a female form of the masculine Robert, of German origin, meaning bright and shining with fame), has been the librarian at the Cranston Public Library, Knightsville branch. Located at 1847 Cranston Street in the city of Cranston, Rhode Island, the city in which we live. In 1960, the United States Government Census Bureau reported the population of Cranston to be 66,766, which my mother says has not increased substantially in the two years since. At least not in our mostly lower-middle-class suburban section of the city, with its quiet tree-lined streets and shady sidewalks and grassy front yards. Its functioning street lamps and single-family bungalow-style houses. Its rivers and streams and fields and ballparks and schools, its train tracks and its tracts of still-forested land, dense enough to hide out in should the need arise. The *town* of Cranston was created back in 1754, being then a collection of neighborhoods in the southern district of the city of Providence (the state's capital), but it did not become an actual city until March 10, 1910. In case you were wondering.

I began my public school education in the second grade at the age of 4, at the John W. Horton Elementary School. Until then my mother had brought me to work with her each day at the library, and so I learned how to read and write at an early age, since there's really nothing else to do—eight hours a day, five days a week, year in year out—in a library.

Not that I'm complaining. Because reading has always been my second favorite thing to do—next to writing—and it has helped me immensely with my writing, as you can imagine. If not so much with my relationships with people. Adults, mainly. The more perplexing variant of our species by far, I'd have to say. I've always known that one day I would become a writer, literary fiction being my main interest. But who knows, after I've aged a bit more and have acquired greater skill and depth and life experience, maybe poetry, too. Plays. Essays. Criticism. Philosophy, even. Anything is possible. This being my first work submitted for publication, however, the day of my becoming a professional writer has officially arrived. Rejections notwithstanding.

As I mentioned, we live in the city of Cranston, in the ethnically diverse neighborhood of Forest Hills. At 44 Brookfield Road to be exact—which I like to be, even though adults will call me out for it, using words like *precocious*, which they think I won't understand. And so I end up having to explain to them that I consider having developed certain abilities and proclivities at an earlier age than usual—and being mature, clever and advanced for my young age—to be a feather in my cap. Which only confirms their point, I suppose, but also gets them off my precocious little ass. Temporarily, at least.

My mother—always supportive—often reminds me that I remind her of herself when she was my age. And that growing up in foster homes made it necessary at times to suppress her intellectual aptitude and interests for the sake of others perhaps less cerebrally endowed (like her current husband, for one sterling example). Suggesting indirectly that I might try and imagine things from the other's point of view myself, which I can see the value of, theoretically. How it requires and so further develops tolerance and compassion and understanding. But actually feeling a genuine desire to see things from the other's point of view (as she can, and does!) remains elusive and beyond my grasp. Especially concerning her current husband.

The closest I can come to voluntarily suppressing my intellectual aptitude is when I sense that the result may be harmful to me if I don't. Such as when interacting with my peers. Out on the street, one must take one's highbrow intellectual aptitude down a notch, or risk being branded a bookworm, a nerd, a sissy, a freak, and so on. To be accepted as normal and non-threatening out there, one must speak in a stereotypical, non-scholarly, age-specific vernacular. Hence, in my case, a two-tiered hierarchy of verbal expression has evolved: (1) academic, and (2) exoteric. In case you were wondering.

Indeed, even at the earliest stages of sociological development, we are instructed in a kind of sandbox socialism, or playground populism, or kiddie communism—call it what you will—under the guise of *let's all try to fit in and get along*, so that the status quo can be duly maintained. I'm all for fitting in, just not mandatorily into what everyone else fits into, as urged in the sophistic maxim: *Be yourself; everyone else is taken.* And I'm all for getting along, too. As long as you get along with me as well as I get along with you.

At least in the company of my mother, Roberta Olsen Seeks, I can relax and be my preferred erudite self. Perhaps with the occasional gentle motherly admonishment, but without fear of rejection or reprisal.

And every now and then, even she will wax lyrical and philosophical.

The world comes crashing into existence anew in each and every moment, Clifford, she once remarked, during a memorable debate we were having on the pros and cons of seeing things from the other's point of view. Bringing with it life itself, she said, with all its multitudinous variety and possibilities. And how incomprehensible the energy must be that is required to do that! she said. With our minds hardly able to remain quiet and still enough to perceive it!

I nodded thoughtfully. (We were in our '52 Galaxie on a pilgrimage to New York to hear a talk by the author, Henry Miller, whose novel, *Tropic of Cancer*—notorious for its candid sexuality, and from which I had learned much about the more lurid aspects of the facts of life—had just been published in the U.S.)

It's an established fact, I said, that our brain limits our capacity to experience ultimate reality, or else we'd be coming apart at the seams every moment, and never get anything done. In and of themselves, I said, these are uber-profound points of view, Mother. But what do they have to do with the argument? With why I should care about seeing things from another's point of view?

Because life itself is the greatest prize, Clifford, she said. That's what these points of view have to do with this discourse. And we've already won it, you and I!

How did we win it? I said. Superior skill? Smarts? Looks? Talent? Charm? By default? By cheating? And again, what's it got to do with—

Because a prize is something you win, dear, she said. Speaking metaphorically, when you realize that life is the greatest prize of all, and that once you've won it you can relax and enjoy *all* of it, then seeing things from the other's point of view is a snap. And if you doubt that life is the greatest prize, just consider the alternative. I mean, where would you be without it?

Dead, I suppose, I said. In which case, nary a point of view would matter.

I prefer nonexistent, she said. Dead would mean you won the prize and then lost it. What I'm saying is, consider, while you *are* alive, where you would be if you had never been alive. She smiled at me. If you had experienced *nary* a blessed thing? Wouldn't you wish you were alive?

Okay then, I said, I agree. In that case, nonexistent is the more appropriate term. I was responding from a more literal perspective.

And nary? she said. Really, Clifford. Last time I checked, this is the middle of the twentieth century. Not the nineteenth.

It was the eighteenth, actually, I said, gazing out at the shipyards as we crossed the Thames in New London. The origin of nary, I mean. Was mid eighteenth century.

She rolled her eyes. Well, can we agree it must have been used in the nineteenth as well, then? We don't need to wear our knowledge and our intellect like a fine new cap all the time, dear. When inside, we can remove it and hang it up with other such useful garments. The point is, we're inexplicably lucky to be alive and anywhere at all. So if it helps us to coexist and get along with others and be happy, why not try and see things from the other's point of view? What's there to lose? Let's celebrate everything, be grateful for all that comes our way, good and bad alike. Including opposing views.

All that comes our way, I said. Literally all.

Yes, literally all.

Bad things, too?

Indeed. Everything.

That doesn't sound right, I said. Or prudent. Or advantageous.

Life isn't supposed to be right, or prudent, or advantageous, Clifford! It just is. Do you want to be right all the time, or do you want to be happy?

I want to be both, I said.

That'll be a small club, dear. How happy do you expect you'll be—alone?

I don't know, Mother. I've never been alone. We've always been alone together. Like now, here. In the car.

You've never been right all the time, either, she said, slowing to shake off a state trooper. No one has, she said.

Well, I expect I'd be happier than if I was wrong and miserable, I said. Like you often seem to be…with him.

If my mother was taken aback by my riposte, she hid it well.

The trick, she said, eyeing me closely, the more efficacious attitude, I should say, is to be grateful for everything we experience. She swerved to avoid the guardrail. Even our differences, she said.

But how? I said. I can see being more accepting of our differences. But… grateful? And Mother, eyes on the road, please.

More accepting is a start, she said. A good one.

But you're saying to be grateful for the bad stuff, too, I said. To be grateful—thankful and appreciative—even if someone harms you?

Well. Of course we try to avoid that.

Sorry, Mother. It sounds misguided. Injudicious. I prefer to reject the bad altogether, in favor of the good.

Then you'll do so at your peril, Clifford. Someday you'll see. It is an unfathomable gift just to be here. And once we are here and breathing comfortably, the prize has been won—so to speak—and life owes us nothing more.

But don't we owe our lives something? I said. Like, to feel safe and secure. To suffer less. To enjoy life more.

That's exactly the point! she said. To enjoy life more we must enjoy more of life, as in, all of it. The good and the bad alike, don't you see?

Really? I said, stuck in doubt. Grateful for the good, and the bad…

I don't expect you to understand right now, she said. It's…subtle.

No fair! I said. Below the belt, that one was.

Perhaps when you're older, dear.

Well, older isn't looking that much better from here, I said. How much older?

Who knows, she said. Minutes. Hours. Days, weeks, years. Older.

I peered at her. You adults, I said, are an uber-cryptic breed.

Well, in that case, Clifford, you are merely a younger and smaller and less-experienced variety of this uber-cryptic breed. And what do you expect you'll eventually grow into?

An uber-cryptic uber debater? I said.

She honked the horn and waved to a gang of motorcyclists passing by. Then she reached over and tousled my hair. I don't doubt you will, she said.

No one can help you, I thought, like a parent can.

No one can harm you like a parent can, either.

I never knew my biological father, but as soon as I was old enough to understand, my mother told me the story. It wasn't until they were married for a while and I was already growing inside her that she realized he was different from the other men she'd known, and that she had misread him grossly. His name was (is?) Godfrey Seeks (a given name from the Old French *Godefroy*, meaning good peace). You may have heard of him or read something he wrote. An investigative journalist, he was published in *Life* magazine. My mother showed me an article he wrote about the Israel Defense Forces (IDF). Fascinating material. Impressive writing, too.

According to my mother, though, my father was much too good looking to be a man. And one day, when she was several months pregnant with me, she woke up and found a note on the dresser saying he was sorry but he couldn't be her husband anymore, and had set out to find one of his own. A husband, that is. Should've known, my mother said. Way too good looking. She said she gave him credit for being honest, though, since it took real guts to admit to being homosexual in Rhode Island in 1948. Or anywhere else in the world for that matter, she said, and in pretty much any other year throughout history, too. Sadly. But don't worry, Clifford, she said to me. Between your father's over-the-top good looks and my subpar ones, you're just good looking enough to be the perfect degree of gorgeous.

Well, I thought. As seen through the eyes of an adoring (if self-deprecating) mother, what young son isn't?

I think I might try and find him someday and have a conversation with him about the writing profession, which we now have in common. He could show me some of his work, and I could show him…this story. And, maybe we could have another conversation, too, about why—queer and gutsy or not—he never once wrote to us or checked up on us in the fourteen years since he abandoned us. I mean, maybe my mother could've used some help. I mean, if we're trying to see things from *the other's point of view.* I mean, who does the queer and gutsy S.O.B. think he is? I mean, unless he's dead. Which is entirely possible, and I can't say it would be a problem for me at all if he was.

Consequently, I was born fatherless and named (rather whimsically, I have to say) after my mother's childhood sweetheart, Clifford Jiles, now the head librarian at the Cranston Public Library, Auburn branch (purely by coincidence). Currently married, with five children of his own, none of which he has abandoned. In case you were wondering.

Now, I can't say that I ever missed having a father, my mother being determined to satisfy all of my parental needs herself. When I turned ten, for instance, she began enrolling me in organized contact sports programs. Innocently, of course, thinking that adult-supervised physical activity on a regular basis with kids my own age would balance my bookishness, and help me grow up happy, and healthy, and confident. Football, ice hockey, basketball, baseball—the very same sports I'd been happily and healthily and confidently playing for years, in unofficial, unorganized, unsupervised, and unselfconscious conditions. I appreciated her concern for my health, happiness and well-being, of course, and I did my utmost best to cope with all the so-called well-meaning adults you encounter in these official leagues. But after two eye-rolling years of organized sports, I have to say, it just wasn't my thing. And so I quit.

Fortunately, there was never a heavy-duty father figure around the house to contend with when making these kinds of critical life-decisions. That is, not until a year ago. When my mother married an organized-con-tact-sports fanatic. One who turned out to be an extremely heavy-duty father figure, and, as I mentioned, a highly accomplished drinker, named Bart Wyfford. (Pronounced Wif-ford, an altered spelling of Wofford, of Anglo-Saxon origin, a habitation surname derived from the names of towns and villages; given name Bartholomew—Bart, the diminutive—of Aramaic origin, meaning rich in land.) Bart told my mother he would adopt me, but only if I joined an official sports league and took his surname as my own. Which would've made my name Clifford Wyfford (pronounced Clifford Wifford). And there was just no way that either of those things was going to happen.

For the past year—up until the incident occurred in which Bart was violently blinded in one eye—he worked nights part-time at the Cranston Print Works. And played what can only be described in technical musical terminology as: exceptionally worthless guitar (*chitarra senza valore*), in an amateur swing-style jazz band called, The Swinging Gates. (Which my occasional best friend, Ziggy Zigarelli, aptly nicknamed The Rusty Gates, as in, swings like a rusty gate). Meaning that Bart was free during the day to harass me about re-joining one of these official leagues.

But as I explained to Bart and to my mother, I'm done with these official leagues.

Official leagues—with their sleazy adult umpires, who from time to time will give the catcher's ass (i.e., mine) a furtive rub or a surreptitious pinch. The licentious freaks.

Official leagues—with their loony adult rules that you can never break in order to give some poor lumpy kid another chance when he obviously needs something to help him hold back the tears. The poor lump.

Official leagues—with their cheering and booing adult spectators, who shouldn't give a damn about the rules of the game when the score is 33 to 0 in favor of the visiting team, and the sport is ice hockey, and all the home team fans departed hours ago.

Official leagues—with their nervy adult parents pushing their absurd expectations and their intimidating advice on their embarrassed and athletically-challenged kids, who will invariably go on to become queer rocket scientists, or queer religious figures, or queer investigative journalists like my father. (Nothing wrong with queer, of course, but religious? Now there's a view of which I will never see the other's point.)

Official leagues—with their cheesy corporate sponsors and their goofy corporate logos, and their too-big-and-baggy-and-zipper-less or too-small-and-tight-and-zipper-less uniforms (apparently designed by eunuchs). And god help you if you don't scour them clean before and after every game.

Official leagues—with their grumpy ice-cream truck vendors parked by the curb, waiting greedily for your quarter, if you're lucky enough to have one. Which I and many of the kids on the teams I played on never were. Because our families have too many financial problems, and not enough fathers with decent jobs who don't drink their pay away.

So, it's neighborhood sports or *no* sports for me. As in, *no* adults. As in, sports played in the street, or in vacant lots, and always in your street clothes. Where, if you're one of the best or biggest or oldest players in your neighborhood, you can be captain of a team, and choose-up with another captain for the players you want. By choosing-up I mean you throw out one or two fingers at the same time the other captain throws out one or two fingers, and as you do you call odds or evens. And if you call the total amount of fingers correctly, you get to choose a player for your team from the gang of kids milling around. Looking as though they can't wait to leave, but are secretly praying they'll get picked before the fateful final round. (You can almost hear them begging the Patron Saint of *Better Luck Next Time*: Please God, don't make me the last one picked. Again.)

And so you and the other captain will continue choosing-up sides like this until every kid present is on one team or another. Even the wonky leftover ones that nobody wants but will always be included. Because this is neighborhood-style sports, not some high-pressure organized league run by creepy, condescending, know-it-all adults, with their quixotic standards.

Not that I'm bitter.

And there are *no* benches in our neighborhood games either, because every kid plays. All the time. Even when there are so many kids on a team that there have to be three pitchers (or quarterbacks or point men) taking turns throwing a pitch. Or a handful of center fielders (or defensemen or linebackers) catching a single fly ball. Or several catchers (or goalies or safeties) backing each other up and chasing after the often-thrilling-but-wildly-off-target throws to home. So many kids, in fact, that the batting rotation can take hours to complete, and you'll be lucky to make it to the plate twice in an entire game.

Sure, it gets crowded and chaotic during these neighborhood games. But at least there are no snarky adult umpires who will throw you out for hurling your bat at the pitcher when he heeds calls from the infield to bean you at the plate. Which he somehow can do with far greater accuracy than when he aims for the strike zone. In fact, in my neighborhood, the closest thing to umping is when both teams do a pig-pile on top of the two players involved in a dispute (usually these players are on different teams, but not always), and whichever player gets out from under the pile and onto his feet first—gets to call it.

Now that's good sportsmanship. And fun.

I realize that I've said "he" and "him" and whichever player gets onto "his" feet first, etc., suggesting a male bias. And perhaps there is a modicum of that on the street. But it's nothing like in the official leagues, where the well-meaning adults in charge have decided that girls should not be allowed to play on boys' teams—only to cheer for them. (And as my mother candidly remarked to our coach, *How Neanderthal is that?*) Neighborhood sports are considerably more progressive and forward-thinking and co-ed. Girls are more than welcome here. Like, for instance, when we need one to even up the sides, or when we need a slew of them so that each team has enough players to have a decent game.

Or, if they happen to be astute players, like Judith Meiselman, for example. Who moved in next-door to me last year, and who Ziggy Zigarelli nicknamed MiserMan, because his mother says that Jews are always saving up their money like misers and buying property and selling it for big profits.

In that case, I said to Ziggy, wouldn't *WiserMan* be a more fitting sobriquet?

You're not serious, Ziggy said. *WiserMan?* For a Jew? In this neighborhood? He scoffed. We got WASPS and Catholics. Jickies and guineas, mostly. Over by the Print Works, we got the mill houses, full of your micks and your polacks, your krauts and frogs. Orientals by the train tracks—your chinks, your nips, your gooks. Russkies down by the river. Real live redskins in the Village—hey, how the hell'd so many Injuns get here, anyway?

I sighed. Because American Indians were here first, Ziggy. Before anyone else. And you left out the Latinos, and the Armenians.

Right, I always forget about the spics and them goat-bangin' towel-heads. Good fielders, though. Thank God we got no coloreds yet, no spoo—

Jesus, Ziggy! I said. Have some respect. Try Negroes! You sound more like an adult every time you open your mouth. This is 1962, in case you lost count. John Fitzgerald Kennedy—an Irish Catholic—is in the White House. Martin Luther King Junior—a black civil rights leader—is raising everyone's consciousness. Except yours. Just because you're so ignorant doesn't give you the right to call people insulting names.

Whatever, Ziggy said. Anyways, he said. No way would *WiserMan* fly for a kike around here.

But wait, I said. Isn't Ziggy a German/Jewish name? Short for Siegfried, or Sigmund, or something like that?

Ziggy almost choked. Shut up, Whacks! he said. It's short for Zigarelli, you dumb dipshit. I'm a goddamn dago, for Christ's sake. And proud of it.

In the end, MiserMan was the moniker that stuck. And it was a gift compared to the other more sophomoric names Ziggy had conjured up. Like MeasleMan. WeaselMan. StinkelMan. And his favorite, FecalMan. (And he calls me a dumb dipshit.) He talks like this because he knows it bothers me. But I've seen him be nice to people of all ethnic and racial backgrounds. There really is a kind and decent—if comatose—heart buried beneath all that bigoted, racist, adult-like xenophobic rhetoric.

Anyway, the girls in our neighborhood are indifferent about being captains, which is fine. Because some of them may be a little too adept at it and end up dominating the game, and taking all the enjoyment and gratification out of it. Plus, no matter what the sport is, there's a lot of rough physical contact involved in the way we play it. And with girls, well, you don't want to have to worry about hurting them and sending them home crying.

Unless, once again, it's somebody like Judith Meiselman. Because she's as powerful as we are. More so, maybe, even though she isn't any bigger. And you simply cannot intimidate her, so you pretty much have nothing to worry about. Except that she will likely beat you. At everything.

Additionally, we play in the street, as I said. Meaning sometimes in traffic. While dodging cars and trucks and motorcycles and these awesome Ethiopian marathon runners from South Providence. Always training for a race. Who once stopped running to tell us—of all things—to be careful while playing in the street! No offense, Ziggy chimed in, but cool and hep as you darkies are, youse are the ones gotta be careful in these here streets. We got wackos to spare around here.

Now, the surfaces we play on are mainly bloodstained concrete or blacktop, or bloodstained hard-packed gravel, and not your soft, cushy, un-bloodstained grass—or (excuse me) *AstroTurf*—which all those sissified league games are played on. And—although I don't like to admit this, I will for the sake of credibility—landing on one of those cement surfaces has even brought a tear or two to my own eyes.

One time, MiserMan landed so hard on Brookfield Road that she tore a patch of skin off her knee the size of a silver dollar. I felt a painful jolt in my groin when I saw that bloody piece of skin hanging by a few thin threads. Froggy LaPorte—the shortest and stoutest kid in the neighborhood, and one you do not want to antagonize, because he will yank you to the ground and sit on you till the street lights come on—even told her to go home and have it looked at.

But MiserMan? She just takes a deep breath, and grits her teeth, and brushes all the pebbles and dirt off of it, and wipes the blood with her shirt, and gets up and keeps on playing. Did not shed one single tear. Although she did run slower than usual, which allowed me to tag her out at home plate after she hit that smoking line drive her next time at bat. The one that bounced off the roof of Mickey O'Rourke's raised rabbit cages (and here Ziggy simply changed the original "N" in Nicky to "M" for Mickey, because Nicky O'Rourke is Irish), and would have been a grand slam for sure. Her second of the game. I almost hated to tag her out and end her reign of terror. But I did.

Judith MiserMan—or Meiselman—is the quintessential neighborhood sportsman (or sportswoman). One tough kid, we all said to each other. When she wasn't standing around listening.

Most of the kids in my neighborhood agree that organized league games are nothing special to play in, and that we're all adequate players and don't need official leagues to prove it in. Or official adults to prove it to. We're athletic, experienced, and fair.

However, if I'm being completely honest, sometimes there's been a problem with *fair*. Like the time MiserMan was pitching and I hit a hard drive that smashed her in the leg and ricocheted off her foot and smacked her on the chin and flew straight into her bare hand, which she raised up high and shook to show us she'd caught the ball. It was just too phenomenal to believe.

So I demanded a do-over (unfairly, I will admit), which caused an all-out riot on the field. Finally, to avoid more bloodshed, MiserMan agreed to redo the play, and proceeded to strike me out with three straight-down-the-middle fastballs which I didn't even see coming.

Sometimes you have to admit that, yes, you too can be an asshole.

As time passed, however, the more enticing thing I noticed about Miser-Man was…her body. Strong, but lithe and supple. Agile. Willowy. Sensual and curvaceous. For a fourteen-year-old girl, uber-rockin'. And when she wore those tight little shorts? Hmm. Forget about keeping your eyes on the ball. A bit shy on top, perhaps. But every time you gazed up there, there was evidence of new growth.

And the fact that she lived next door to me—and that our houses were a mere nine feet seven-and-a-half inches apart, and the window in her bedroom faced the window in mine, and sometimes she'd forget to pull the shade down and close the curtains—was one I found increasingly alluring.

When school resumed this past September, MiserMan asked me a question I was reticent to answer. We were walking home on opposite sides of the street, as usual, and she waved to me.

Hey! she called. W-A-X. How'd you get a name like Wax?

Here we go, I muttered. I don't know, I said. How did you get a name like MiserMan?

She smirked. You know perfectly well how I got it, she said. Ziggy Zigarelli. That dumb dipshit.

I nodded. Yeah, I know. He gave me mine, too. He gives them out to everybody. Friend and foe alike.

He's such a dipshit, she said. But…Wax? How can that be? Your name is Clifford Seeks.

Right, I said. Go figure. Ziggy's on a whole other level of dip when it comes to that shit.

Yeah, but W-A-X? she said. Where'd he get that from?

I looked up at the sky, all vast and clear and blue. But inside my head things were cramped, and fogged-in, and gray.

You don't want to know, I said.

She stopped walking. Oh, I don't? she said. Like all of a sudden, *you* know what *I* want? Okay then, she said. *Why* don't I want to know?

I stopped walking and stared at her. So easy on the eyes, she was. I thought about my mother, falling for my father because he was so hand—

Never mind, she said. I know why. You're embarrassed.

I am not, I said. I'm just not going to tell you from way over here.

She looked both ways and started crossing the street just as Mickey O'Rourke's older brother Billy—who Ziggy had long ago christened Bully—barreled around the corner on his new three-speed 28-inch English Racer and rode up behind her and smacked her hard on the butt, yelling *hubba-hubba!* like the cretin that he is. (I hate bullies in general, but Bully O'Rourke specifically. Second only to Bart Wyfford.) So Judith held up her hand and stretched out a tall slim middle finger and flipped Bully off the whole time it took her to strut seductively across the street, bringing to my face the first fully qualified smile of the day.

When she got onto the sidewalk she stood in front of me with her arms folded and looked me in the eye.

How about from here then? she said.

I looked up at the sky again. Felt the drain on my brain again.

It's not W-A-X, I said, quietly. It's W-H-A-C-K-S.

Whacks? she said, looking even more confused.

My mother's husband, Bart, I said. He's always saying he's gonna whack me one if I do this, whack me one if I do that. Whack me one if I do anything. Or if I don't do anything.

So what? she said. Every father says that.

So, one day Ziggy was over, I said. The Cowboys were playing the Patriots. Seconds left in the game, the score's tied. Cowboys' ball on the goal

37

line. And Bart says to me, I'm gonna whack you one if the Pats don't win this. All smiles. Then he says, I'm gonna whack you one if they lose, too.

I thought he was going for a joke, but the next thing I know, he whacks me one, two, three times a charm, making it look like some kind of sick game he's playing. Ziggy's laugh turns nervous. Then the Cowboys score and the Patriots lose, and Bart grabs me and starts whacking away. Ziggy almost vomited he was so scared.

Judith stood shaking her head. I felt the anger boiling inside me, bubbling up like lava, ready to blow.

So, I said. Ziggy started calling me Whacks. And, of course, it stuck.

Judith had turned her head away and was staring down the street in the direction of our houses, her jaw on her chest.

Those jerks, she said. Ziggy. Your father.

Unofficial stepfather, I corrected. Hell, I should've known better, I said. You don't accidentally step in front of the TV set and cause a registered reject like Bart Wyfford to miss the deciding play of the game and not expect to take a few for the team. I sighed. His favorite target by the way? Your nuts. But any old spot where the world can't see the results will do.

Judith reached out and touched my arm consolingly. Son-of-a-bitch, she said, her eyes bugging out like eggs. Then she said, My father's tough, too. He's IDF. Israel Defense Forces. He'd never hit me, though. In fact, I pity the poor jerk who does.

I peered at her. Your father? I said, incredulous. Is Mossad?

Was, she said. He quit after my mom died. Counterterrorism. Covert Ops unit. Uber-dangerous. She eyed me. How do you know about Mossad?

My real father, I said. He wrote an article once, and… Never mind, I said. It's not important.

Judith looked away. Just say the word, she said. My father will teach yours a lesson he'll never forget.

God, no! I said. I might as well sign my own death warrant.

Just then Mr. Meiselman pulled around the corner in his station wagon and stopped at the curb across the street and called to Judith. A dark-skinned man wearing a black beret was sitting in the front seat with him.

Whoa, I gotta go, I said, and took off down the sidewalk.

Whacks, wait! she called. I mean…Clifford!

When I got home I saw the pile of empties in the front yard next to a pile of newly cut grass. A rake was leaning against the house. I figured Bart must have drunk what he'd brought outside with him and gone inside for more. Suddenly I heard a strange whimpering coming from the O'Rourkes' house across the street. Then someone calling for help. I dropped my school books on the front porch and hurried over and peeked into the O'Rourkes' backyard and saw Bully, sitting on top of Ziggy Zigarelli's chest, his knees pinning Ziggy's shoulders to the ground. Ziggy's face was wedged between Bully's legs, and twisting wildly from side to side. Bully had his dick out and it looked like he was about to use it.

I ran up behind him. Bully, I cried. What are you doing? Let him go.

Help me, Whacks! Ziggy screamed. Stop him. Don't let him—

I caught this guinea grease ball trying to take my bike for a ride, Bully yelled. Without permission. He's gonna pay for that.

Not like this he isn't, I said. Get off him.

Bully hocked up a wad of phlegm and spit it in Ziggy's face.

Now! I said.

Fuck off, Whacks.

Let him up, Bully, you asshole!

Bully swung out a long, fat, fifteen-year-old arm and caught me in the mouth with a hard backhand. Lying on the ground with my face on fire and my mouth filling with blood, I looked up and saw Bully on his knees, his dick in Ziggy's face. I scrambled to my feet and brought back my kicking leg and let him have my best shot straight to the kidneys. Bully screamed and buckled over and rolled on the ground. I pulled Ziggy up and we got out of there. Out of the corner of my eye I spotted Mr. Meiselman pulling into his driveway, Judith and the dark-skinned man in the car with him.

We headed for the relative safety of my yard, where Bart was raking the lawn. But as I ran past him, Bart whacked me behind the head hard and sent me flying into the front of the house. I turned around and saw Bully lumbering across the street, Ziggy frozen in place and staring open-mouthed at Bart. Bart standing with his arm outstretched.

Go fight him, you pussy! Bart yelled, standing over me. Get up and go fight him!

I could smell the booze on his breath.

ALL THAT COMES OUR WAY

Else it'll be *me* you fight, he hollered.

Bully arrived and Ziggy screamed and took off, with Bully giving chase.

Get up and go fight that fat mick bastard right now! Bart yelled. Then he lunged for me.

I ducked under him and raced into the backyard and over to the six-foot cyclone fence and started climbing for my life. But Bart was too quick. He grabbed me by the pants and threw me to the ground and stepped on my leg so I couldn't move. Then he brought back his hand and let me have it.

I covered my head with my arms and took the first blow. The second. By the third one I was seeing stars.

Then I heard a high-pitched squeal coming from somewhere. I opened my eyes and saw Mr. Meiselman holding Bart by the wrist and bending his middle finger back into an unnatural position.

Say you'll not hurt the boy again, I heard Mr. Meiselman say. Firmly but politely, as though telling Bart to pass the salt.

Bart was howling in pain. His finger twisted backwards and looking totally wrong.

Say it, Mr. Meiselman said, louder. Or I'll do them all. One by one.

Okay! Bart yelled. Goddamn you! Okay.

Not okay, Mr. Meiselman said. You'll not hurt the boy again. Say it! He squeezed Bart's finger.

Bart screamed. I won't…I won't hurt him…

Never again, Mr. Meiselman said. Say it. Never. Again.

Owww! Shit! Fuck! Never again! Never again!

Mr. Meiselman let Bart's finger go and then he grabbed him by the throat. You do, he said, and your eyes will be next.

To my utter amazement, Bart did not report Mr. Meiselman to the police. Instead, he told my mother that he fell on the stairs and broke his finger, which she did not for one moment believe. She told him if he didn't stop drinking excessively and being abusive to me, she would leave him.

But the threatening looks Bart sent my way over the next few weeks had me wondering how seriously he was taking Mr. Meiselman's warning. And my mother's ultimatum. With his right hand wrapped in that plaster cast, though, I figured there would be precious few whacks to my private parts to have to worry about for a while. At least from that hand.

Meanwhile, Judith and I were getting cozier. Talking through our bedroom windows at night. Walking home from school together every day. Taking a route through the woods to avoid the neighborhood watchdogs.

One day we were sitting in a pine grove making out, getting more hot and bothered by the second. I slipped my hand under her shirt and waited. Got the green light. Then I moved to her bra and cupped my hand over her breast. Waited. Good to go. Then something made me stop.

You sure you're okay with this? I said.

Judith took a breath. What do you think, she said, about us…screwing?

You mean intercourse? I said. Copulation? I said. Fornication, I mean, since we're not married? I paused. Two things, I said. Has to be consensual. Have to use a prophylactic.

Consensual, she said. Meaning *I* have to say yes.

I nodded.

Prophylactic, she said. Meaning *you* have to wear a safety.

I nodded again.

She giggled. You're such a brainiac, Seeks, she said, slapping me on the arm.

Me, a brainiac? I said. You're the one in the Accelerated Division. With perfect grades. In every subject.

She peered at me. Why do you hate school so much? she said. You're the smartest person I've ever met. A natural wiz.

I don't know, I said. It's boring. I could be working on a novel. Winning the Pulitzer.

But you could be doing that anyway, she said.

I looked away. Maybe I am, I said. Maybe I will.

She brought her hand to my chin and turned my head toward her. Maybe you'd better, she said. Then, treating me to a coy smile, Would you ever…want to…go down on me?

I stiffened. Cunnilingus? I said. Like in Miller's *Tropic of Cancer*? Um. Sure. You might have to guide me a little, but…

Judith's grin went wide. Do you have a four-syllable word for everything? she said.

I don't, I said. The English language does. I eyed her. What about you? I said. Would you ever…go down on me?

She slapped me again. A blow job, you mean? I bet you've got a word for that, too.

Four syllables? I said. That would be…fellatio. Oral stimulation of a man's penis.

Or a hot boy's, she said. Hey, she said. Fellatio and cunnilingus. Sounds like a couple of ancient Greek philosophers!

I laughed. More like explorers, I said. When you think about it.

Judith let out a belly-laugh, her hand covering her mouth.

Now will you blow me? I said.

Only if you make me, she said.

It's no fun if I have to make you, I said. That would really suck.

Ha! she said, doubling over. Nice one!

Nice one? I said, reaching for my belt buckle. You want to see a nice one? I'll show you a nice one.

Judith placed her hand on my arm and looked me up and down. She smiled dreamily and lay back in the bed of pine needles and gently pulled me to her. She lifted her skirt up and took my hand and placed it between her legs and closed them around it, a soft moan escaping her lips. Her underwear was already damp, I was thrilled to discover. And all to my credit. Then she ran her hand behind my belt and sank it down to where it was also damp, or wet, rather—okay, soaked—and all to her credit. She moaned again and put her other arm around my neck and pulled me in close and we kissed. Things started getting hot and bothered all over again, and suddenly she broke away.

You sure you're okay with this? she said, stifling a laugh.

Be gentle, I quipped. Go easy. Please. Whilst screwing my brains out.

Judith leaned in and put her lips to my ear. It is a nice one, she said. You're the nicest boy ever, Clifford Seeks.

Back on Planet Earth—aka Brookfield Road—Bully O'Rourke had not forgotten about my kick and had been threatening to get even, promising to retaliate at a moment when I least expected it. I had no idea what sort of evil he was planning, but just the idea of it was enough to keep me hyper vigilant.

Bully let a few weeks pass, until a day came when I was in bed with a cold. Unbeknownst to me, or to Judith, he followed her after school. As luck would have it, Bart had run out of cigarettes and made me get out of bed, coughing and sneezing, and go up the street to Kazminski's Market. On the way home I stole into the woods, hoping to find Judith in the pine grove. But instead, I came upon Bully, sitting on top of Judith's chest. Pinning her shoulders to the ground with his knees, the way he'd done with Ziggy. Muffling her screams with the shirt he'd ripped off her.

I crept up behind him. You just won't learn, will you, Bully, I said.

Bully turned to look and I hauled off and kicked him in the back. Same spot as before, only harder. Much harder. That was my girl he was assaulting this time. And this time, when Bully rolled over, groaning in pain, I made sure he wasn't getting up. I kicked him again as hard as I could. I kicked him for every whack I'd ever taken from Bart Wyfford. For every time a cursed umpire had grabbed my ass. For every phone call and letter I never got from gutsy Godfrey Seeks. I kicked Bully and all those other sons of bitches until Judith made me stop, and Bully lay there unmoving and silent. I grabbed Judith's clothes and helped her on with them, and then we took off. Thinking maybe Bully was dead.

The police came to my house and questioned me about it, and Judith came over with her father and explained what had happened. Mr. Meiselman sat on the ancient yellow Naugahyde sofa in our living room, directly across from Bart, eyeing him. Fuming quietly. Bringing his finger to the corner of his eye every now and then, and tapping it lightly. A not-so-subtle reminder: *Your eyes will be next.*

Bart tried in vain to avoid his hostile stares.

The cops didn't doubt Judith, saying that Bully had been caught doing this kind of thing before. They said he was still in the hospital, and when he recovered he'd likely be going straight to the Sockanosset School for Boys (aka *The Bad Boy School*—an infamous juvenile detention facility in Cranston that housed the worst underage hoodlums in the state, where Bully would no doubt get a good taste of his own medicine). But at least at Sockanosset he would be safe from Mr. Meiselman, whose reaction to the cops' announcement was clearly one of disappointment. You could tell he wanted payback, his pound of flesh, taken with his own hand.

When I heard the word Sockanosset I cringed, knowing that to be sent there was every adult's worst threat, and every boy's worst nightmare. Suddenly I felt sorry for Bully, and even more inexplicably, for Bart, and my father, imagining the anguish they must be suffering on the inside to behave the way they did on the outside. And not just imagining it this time, but feeling it—finally—from the other's damaged point of view.

No one can help you—or harm you—I thought, like you can.

By the start of the next baseball season, Bart had convinced my mother that I should join a supervised league team to improve my hitting and fielding, which were never up to Bart's standards. Or my own for that matter. And so, to keep peace at home and show my mother that I was indeed trying to see things from the other's point of view—trying to be grateful for all that comes my way—I put aside my contempt for organized sports and acquiesced.

The team was decent enough, although I could never relax and enjoy playing in an official league game. Not with all those well-meaning adults poisoning the scene, scrutinizing and advising and criticizing. With Bart always the loudest and meanest of the lot. And so, I played poorly. So poorly that the coach asked me if I would forfeit my playing time to the newest member of the team. A stellar hitter and fielder by the name of—yup, you guessed it: Judith Meiselman. This was patently against all official rules, of course, and so, to Bart's great displeasure, I consented.

Then Bart announced that if I didn't play he would sue the league for allowing a girl to play on a boys' team. So the coach stuck me out in deep right field, a desolate region of the physical plane to which fewer balls had been hit than any other location since time immemorial. A place so off the grid that little damage to the score, if any, could be done. Even by me.

Additionally, a section of the right field fence at the rear of our home ball field had been vandalized—flattened, that is—courtesy of a tribe of troublemakers known as Bully O'Rourke. Immediately beyond the right field fence, the field formed a steep downward slope that ended at the bank of a shallow stream, around which hearty native skunk cabbages grew profusely and gave the stream its colloquial name: Stink River.

Now, according to legend, in the epic final game of my organized-sports career, in the top of the sixth inning, and almost dusk, I had been standing out in right field for half an hour due to batter after batter being walked by our third-string substitute pitcher. And, after drinking nearly a quart of lemonade in the dugout during the previous home-team at-bats, I never had to wiz so badly before in my entire life.

Taking everything into account—being practically invisible out in the boondocks of deep right, twisting at the waist with my legs crossed to staunch the torrent of bodily fluids about to burst out of me, singing made-up verses of the Star Spangled Banner to take my mind off the tribulations of my urinary tract (*Oh-oh say don't you pee…*)—I was confident I wouldn't be missed. And so, with my eyes fixed on the bleachers, I began inching my way backwards toward the opening in the fence—never so grateful for the misdeeds of Bully O'Rourke. And when I reached the end of the field, I turned and bounded through the opening and slid down the gravel bank to the stream and yanked down my zipper-less uniform pants and released a veritable stream of my own.

And as I stood there heaving an ecstatic sigh of relief, I heard the faint boink of a bat and the distant roar of the crowd, and four panic-stricken seconds later a baseball dribbled by and rolled into the water.

I jumped into the stream and grabbed the ball, forgetting that my pants were still down around my knees and the contents of my bladder still pouring out. I scrambled up the slope, my exposed member slapping powerlessly against my legs, spraying me wildly with my own liquified waste—like an untethered fire hose at full blast (only shorter). And I hurled the ball to the astonished centerfielder—yup, you guessed it: Judith Meiselman.

Back in the dugout, sitting in my self-soiled uniform, reeking of urine and skunk cabbage and nursing a desecrated ego, I thought for sure that Bart and the coaches and the umpires and the crowd and the players and the whole sentient universe—everyone except my mother and Judith and Mr. Meiselman—would surely die from laughter. Which would have been just fine with me.

That's how bad it was. In case you were wondering.

But even the darkest cloud has a silver lining, as evidenced by Bart Wyfford's startlingly unexpected show of empathy. The sober words of comfort and consolation he spoke in the car on the way home were proof to me that, at some point in his own life, he had needed to hear those very words himself. And that maybe he didn't get to hear them. And that maybe that's what had led him so far astray. And that no one—at least not Bart Wyfford—went entirely astray.

A week later the For Sale sign went up next-door, and Judith came over to break the bad news. Her father had gotten a new job, they were moving to New York. Bart had seen the sign too, of course. He waited till she left the house (crying), and then—solidly off the wagon now, and to hell with empathy and compassion—he said to me, It's over, Valentino. You're all mine now.

I prayed to the Patron Saints of Battered Boys, and Broken Hearts, and Blue Balls, that the house wouldn't sell.

It sold the next day. To friends of Mr. Meiselman's.

Screw all Patron Saints, I thought. They're just not paying attention.

I'll always remember the look on Judith's face, the sadness in her eyes, the quiver in her bottom lip. The way she stoically sat in the way-back of her father's Country Squire station wagon—her perfectly scarred chin (where my line drive had whacked it) resting on her perfectly scarred knee (where she'd whacked it falling on Brookfield Road)—and accepted her plight. A true champion all the way. Her hand splayed out on the rear window, reaching for me, as her father pulled the Squire behind the moving van and they drove away.

Bart and my mother were watching from the porch, standing apart from one another, my mother cupping her elbows in her hands, hugging herself as though chilled. Looking tired. Worried. And older than she is from too many choices made out of quiet desperation.

Ziggy Zigarelli and Mickey O'Rourke, lolling at the curb. Snickering. Somehow finding mirth in the occasion. The dumb dipshits.

Me, standing alone in the middle of the street. Holding a baseball bat and unable to lift my arm up to wave goodbye. Watching the Squire grow smaller, and biting my lip to keep from losing it outwardly, like I'd already lost it inwardly.

I suddenly felt as though a lifetime's worth of betrayal had been lumped into the fourteen short years I'd been here. As though all of us were irretrievably lost. My mother, my father, Bart, me, Ziggy, Bully. And what was worse, I couldn't think of anything to do about it. Except what we have always done. Endure.

Life is the greatest prize… Maybe.

As the now tiny speck of the Meiselmans' car turned the corner onto Reservoir Avenue and disappeared—my guess is, forever—Ziggy and Mickey came over and stood on either side of me and took turns reminding me what a great player she was. What a great body she had. What a winner she was, and what a loser I would go back to being now that she was gone. Then they each gave my shoulder a collegial tap, and left me there. Alone.

Clifford, I'd like you in before the street lights come on tonight, my mother said from the porch. A wet-blanket weariness in her voice.

I turned around and looked at her. She glanced at Bart.

We three have some unpleasant business to discuss, she said.

Then she stepped inside and closed the door behind her.

Finally, I thought. The other's point of view be damned.

Bart stumbled down the porch steps, shaking his head and chuckling to himself. He slithered into the street and then up next to me and put his arm around my shoulder.

I felt my hand tighten around the bat handle.

It's a back-a square one nows'a what-a is, he slurred.

Old booze-breath, with the latest scoop.

Eyeing the front door and watching for my mother, Bart slid his hand—his good one—up to my neck and took a swath of skin tightly between his thumb and forefinger.

I felt my hand bring the bat behind me and start to raise it.

As he twisted the skin and delivered a painful pinch that caused me to squirm in his grip, a car pulled into the Meiselmans' driveway and honked.

Startled, Bart stopped pinching me but held me there, and together we watched a dark-skinned man wearing a black beret get out of the car and walk over and stand on the sidewalk in front of our house.

Bart eyed him. Then me. Then the bat in my hand.

The man scowled at Bart and shook his head in disapproval. He pointed a finger at his own eye, then at Bart.

Remember, the man said, softly. Never again.

Screw you! Bart said. Who-a fuck you think you—

Don't worry, the man said, looking at me and rolling up his sleeve. You won't need that bat. I'll be here to remind him. Every day. In case he forgets.

I blinked. Could it be? I thought. The new neighbors? The IDF? The Patron Saints of Unanswered Prayers to the rescue?

Bart's face grew dark. Then uncertain. Then he yanked the bat from my hand and shoved me aside.

The man took a step closer, still pointing at his eye, the warning clear: *Your eyes will be next.*

You'll not hurt the boy again, he said, louder.

Bart cowered, and then he grabbed me and raised the bat high.

Never again! the man said, heading straight for us. Say it!

INCIDENT AT PONDEROSA EAST

Roccanne types up a post like this one first thing every morning, her stubby scarred fingers flying over the computer keyboard with the accuracy and grace of a concert pianist. And then she prints it out in big bold letters and hangs it on the fridge in the kitchen and on the walls in the dining area, so we'll all see it and can't say we didn't *realize*.

ATTENTION!

RESIDENTS OF PONDEROSA EAST

IN CASE YOU DIDN'T REALIZE

TODAY IS THURSDAY, MAY 23, 2019

IF YOU CAN SEE THIS NOTICE YOU ARE HERE

" * "

IF THERE IS SOMEWHERE *ELSE*
YOU NEED TO BE TODAY

SPEAK UP!

She might as well add what she's thinking: YOU MORONS!

Something dreadful must've happened somewhere along the way—in the birth canal, during conception, a previous incarnation—to make her so damn ornery. This date-posting thing she does, with the flippant commentary, has to do with us residents missing our scheduled appointments—be they medical, legal or otherwise—because we forgot what day it is, and Roccanne was too busy to check her calendar and remind us. For which she ultimately takes the heat, because she's the one responsible for getting us there. Not for driving us there herself—she's too ornery for that; just for making sure somebody does. Some unlucky staff person or volunteer.

And she takes it personally when we screw up, which is crazy because… well…*we're* crazy. Or else we wouldn't be here. Not so much in my case, unless you count lazy as crazy. But the others for sure. Including—once upon a time—Roccanne herself.

Last week it was **WEDNESDAY, MAY 15, 2019** for three straight days. Might still be **WEDNESDAY, MAY 15, 2019** if I didn't SPEAK UP!—like her snooty sign says.

Roccanne was at her desk in the front office, typing madly away, attacking the keyboard as though each key was one of us. A resident. The enemy. I got her attention by waving my arms and pointing to the wall. She halted her assault and yanked out an earbud and scowled.

What is it, *now?* she said.

Now who doesn't realize? I said, holding her **MAY 15, 2019** post in one hand and a calendar in the other. Now who forgot what date it is?

She glared at me over her computer screen and raised a plump spongy hand, fingers splayed, the dirt under her fingernails visible across the room.

Know what this is? she said.

Looks like the back of your hand, I said. Or a worn-out pincushion.

It's this times five, she said, closing all her fingers except the middle one. Letting it stand there, short and erect, while she resumed typing up the dinner menu with her other hand. Slapping the keys with quick and deadly sniper shots straight to our heads. Delivered with surgical precision, straight from the heart. It looked like something she'd practiced.

Here we go, I said. Rock 'n rollin' with Roccanne Roland.

Die alone, Kool, she said.

Another thing you have to *realize* here at Ponderosa East, is that Roccanne used to be a cutter. Used to shoot herself full of junk daily, too. But somehow—with Jerry's help—she managed to kick the habit and all the bad stuff that went with it. Except for the attitude, which she has definitely not kicked. Nonetheless, she's Jerry's all-time-favorite-come-from-behind-victory story. No new wounds lately either, not on the parts of her you can see, at least. Not that she tries to hide them, or the Swiss Army pocket knife she uses to make them. Her only vice now is rock 'n roll—that single-cell sonic pollutant resulting from melody, harmony and rhythm being combined in soul-damaging ways, by those with minimal-to-no musical knowledge, talent, or ability. Exceptions noted. Being a professional musician myself—playing piano for over half a century and studying all the classics and all styles of jazz, even teaching privately during a slow spell some thirty years ago (middle-school-age kids, mostly, huge waste of time)—it's understandable why I'd be critical of such lowbrow taste. Thankfully, Jerry shares my bias. So, while on the premises of Ponderosa East, Roccanne must listen to that sorrowful anti-art through her earbuds. Which she keeps—along with her pocket knife—in a coffee mug on her desk.

In her defense, I must admit that things do get over-the-top nutty around here. On a daily—even hourly—basis. I'm talking round-the-clock, howling-at-the-moon, Looney-Tunes-style batty bonkers. Currently there are four of us residents living in this private home owned by Dr. Jerome Weisberg. Five, if you count Jerry himself, and you might as well. A licensed clinical social worker and psychotherapist turned wannabe jazz guitarist. (Emphasis on wannabe.) A psycho-jazz-guitar-apist, I call him. Himself a model of recovery. Opioids. The mega hard stuff. He's been clean now for over a decade, but not without incurring some basic socio-neurological wear and tear. Including issues with hygiene and flatulence.

Jerry calls this place Ponderosa East—after the horse ranch on the old TV Western series, *Bonanza*. Even though it's nothing close to a rambling trillion-acre spread in the heart of the Old West, but a crumbling three-story Victorian with cone-shaped spires perched like missiles aimed at the sky. Located across from the high school on Park Avenue in the city of Cranston, Rhode Island, which is about as far east as you can get and still be in the continental USA. Built in 1899, Ponderosa East was first remodeled in 1929, then again in '59, again in '89, and so is due sometime this year for a fourth facelift in keeping with the traditional thirty-year span between renovations. Meaning, there's still a few walls standing that haven't yet tumbled down around us.

At my first therapy session with Jerry a year ago, he said he had purchased my book on jazz improvisation back when it debuted some thirty years prior, and was still practicing from it. Still trying to learn how to improvise—how to play jazz on the guitar. I thought, Well, if he hasn't figured it out by now...after thirty years... But some never do. Like those middle-school kids I tried to teach. Who never practiced. Lost causes, really. Regardless of the level, you can't help them if they don't practice. And then the parents—the dads mostly, the moms might cut you a break—blame the teacher. Me, in this case. Which did not help my confidence or self-esteem any, speaking of lost causes. The only thing it ever helped was my drinking and my drugging and my blackout-ing. Good thing I stopped. Teaching, I mean. Drinks, drugs, blackouts and moms are another story. Hard to remember much of anything from back then. Probably another good thing.

Doctor Jazz-berg and I met twice a week for a few weeks in an attempt to help me quit or curb—I'd have even settled for ignore—my addictions. But I couldn't continue any longer than that because his fee was cutting into my troubled finances and threatening my ability to support the very habits I was trying to kick. A total deal-breaker for me. So Jerry suggested we barter: jazz lessons for head sessions. Improvisation for analyzation. Adding that we would have to do it on the QT, since fraternizing with a patient in this manner breaks the professional psychotherapy code of ethics. I said *great*, figuring it would enable me to continue to work on the problem via therapy sessions, while staying sufficiently high to endure them.

But after two months of no gigs—not a single post-funeral party (which had become my main source of income after the arthritis started attacking my hands, and through them the piano)—my funds dried up completely, and so I had to quit therapy. Jerry was disappointed. He had just started making miraculous—albeit basic—progress with his jazz playing, due in large part to my coaching. (See kids, I'm not the boogeyman after all. Not if you practice. I'm the boogie-woogie man. Or used to be.)

The very next day, Jerry called me up and said that with certain clients he offers an all-expenses-paid roof over their head once they run out of family or money or both, and he invited me to move in and become a resident of Ponderosa East, like the others. He said he'd always wanted to do something good with his inheritance, and this is what he chose to do. And that the deal would remain solid as long as we kept up our counseling sessions, and I tutored him with his jazz playing. And that if I ever got sober—or if he ever got a steady full-time jazz gig (of which there had not been one anywhere in the known universe never mind in the state of Rhode

Island since the 60s, and certainly not for someone with Jerry's musical issues)—we'd revisit the arrangement. With my problems being about as bad as Jerry's playing, I understood this to mean that—should I accept his invitation—Ponderosa East would likely be my home from here on out.

Since I couldn't recall having any family left (maybe there was somebody two or three times removed somewhere in Baton Rouge, or was it Boca Raton?), and since my experience with money had always been hallucinatory (here one minute, gone the next) if not magical (now you see it, now you don't), I once again said *great*, and grabbed my piano and my music and my LPs and CDs and BVDs and became a resident.

Jerry lives alone on the third floor of Ponderosa East, while we residents have our own private rooms on the second, each with a window and (yes!) a private bath; with the front office, kitchen, dining area and rec room all on the first floor. The place is drafty and cold in winter (we keep our undergarments doubled up day and night). Stifling hot in summer (we sit half naked—careful about which half—under the sprinkler from dawn to dusk). But just perfect in the spring and fall. Except that that's when the hordes of kids at the high school across the street think it's perfect also, and set about proving it to every adult within annoying distance.

Currently, the paint's peeling, the pipes and windows are leaking, the floors are creaking, and the stairs are whining—which Jerry would argue is nothing compared to how the residents are peeling and leaking and creaking and whining. But the price is right, and there's plenty of psychodrama to keep you throwing off the covers every morning. If you told me back when I first wrote that book on jazz improvisation that something like this would've come of it, I would've shook my head and ordered us another round—doubles they would've been—and kept them coming.

The staffers who run Ponderosa East are all former clients of Jerry's. Graduates, he calls them. There's Roccanne, who you've met—our house director and Chief Executive Angry Bitch; Otto—our cook and Chief Executive Handy Person (Otto's motto: I Make It, You Eat It; You Break It, You Fix It); and Katerina—our housekeeper and Chief Executive Immigration Officer Dodger.

They'd all rather be doing something else, and usually are. So I keep my own calendar on the wall in my room. Sexy little thing. For assurance purposes. Mostly. And so I don't fail to *realize*.

ATTENTION!
RESIDENTS OF PONDEROSA EAST
IN CASE YOU DIDN'T REALIZE
TODAY IS TUESDAY, JUNE 4, 2019
IF YOU CAN SEE THIS NOTICE YOU ARE HERE
" * "

IF THERE IS SOMEWHERE *ELSE*
YOU NEED TO BE TODAY
SPEAK UP!
AND FOR THE LAST TIME,
DON'T EXPECT ME TO CARE
ABOUT YOU AND YOUR PROBLEMS
MORE THAN YOU DO!

Way to frame the argument, Roccanne, I thought. Maybe we crazies don't care about our problems because we don't *realize* we have any. None except for ornery old you, that is.

By mid-afternoon on this fateful day, Jerry and I and the other residents were sitting in the rec room, with Doctor Phil blah blahin' away on TV (it was Jerry's turn to hold the remote), and out of nowhere appeared this attractive new face in the doorway.

Hello everyone, she said, popping her head into the room. Bright, nervous smile. I'm Olive Fuller. Your new meditation facilitator.

Jerry killed the TV. Whoops, he said. Eh…so good of you to come.

She eyed him. I trust Dr. Weisberg told you all I'd be coming by today?

Whoops, Jerry said, again. I suppose I guess I maybe forgot to mention it. But now that you're here, dear…please, come right in. We love a visitor.

She walked over to the upright piano in the corner and stood beside the full-length mirror hanging on the wall behind her to her left. Mid forties. Average height. Hot bod. Silvery blond hair pulled back in a ponytail. She wore a knee-length tie-dyed orange and red sarong with cloth sandals, and smelled of fresh-cut flowers and patchouli oil. Her left eye was wrapped in a murky trombone-yellow birthmark that tapered off toward her left ear. Something looked familiar about it, besides the color.

I caught her attention and nodded hello. Scratched an itch I didn't feel on my left cheek, not meaning to. She looked away and set her backpack down on the piano bench.

All my friends call me Liv, she said. You folks can, too.

Friends already, I thought. That was quick.

Meditation is my medication, she said, putting a sultry little rhythmic bounce in her delivery.

Cool, I thought.

Her name lingered in my mind. Olive Fuller. Liv, to her friends. And then I realized.

So, I said. Liv Fuller, meditation facilitator. As in, by meditating we can live fuller?

Yes, she said, avoiding my gaze. That's correct.

Keeping things formal, I thought.

She bent over and opened her backpack and began rummaging though it. Breasts swinging braless behind the thin cotton fabric of her dress. Nipples poking out like dancing doorbells. I could almost hear the classic cadence of a major 3rd interval chiming away: Ding-Dong.

I watched her take us all in, one at a time, her eyes landing first on Jerry—unshaven and wrapped in his striped terry cloth bathrobe, lounging in a turquoise Naugahyde recliner, half-closed eyes slanting downwards at the corners. Short graying tufts of hair spiked every which way, still wet from his shower. His bony fingers clasped over a bloated belly, his bare feet bearing unsightly long and yellowed toenails, his mouth turned upwards naturally at the ends, presenting a misleading smile.

Next, the Reverend Mary Kreapy—spilling out of a rickety Bentley rocker positioned off to the left behind Jerry, her cold sunken eyes grilling Liv suspiciously. Bundled up in a full-length quilted housecoat, buttoned to the neck, the scars from multiple surgeries escaping beyond the reach of a pale-pink bathing cap adorned with colorful latex flowers. Once an ordained minister, she'd survived a stroke that produced a previously unknown form of coprolalia, causing victims to shout insults and inappropriate language using words that began with the same letter. A tough sell in church.

On to Cora Eaton—a former art critic and a super-sized regular at the McDonald's on the corner of Park and Reservoir, wearing soiled sweats and a mustard-stained T shirt, her corpulence splayed across a wicker sofa on the verge of collapse. Ponderosa East's self-proclaimed QBGTL sweetheart. Uncertain about her sexuality as a boy scout (Q)—so she'll explain to all who inquire—he/she went both ways for a while (B), until falling hard for Nathan (G), then crossing over to become Cora (T), only to find true love with Cynthia and Linda and Vanessa (L)—bringing new meaning and order to the acronym LGBTQ. With the rear half of her head shaved bare, and the front half covered in bangs down to her nose, she lay studying the ceiling while drool collected on her numerous chins.

Squatting on the floor in her ballet costume—cross-legged and cross-eyed in front of the TV—was four-foot-ten and wafer-thin Irma Stank, her bales of curly locks dyed fire-engine red and stuffed into a bulging hairnet. Once a bank teller at Washington Trust Savings and Loan, stood up by the groom on her wedding day a decade ago, swatting spindly arms at an imaginary suitor she called Ike.

Then to ornery Roccanne Roland—a former beauty pageant runner-up (Miss Teen Rhode Island, 2001), earbuds dug in deep, pocket knife dangling from her belt. Slouching listlessly against the door to her office, while inspecting the scores of little raised welts on her forearms. Each ridge, each cut, each slice, telling its own desperate story.

And finally, Liv's gaze swept—rather curtly—over me, Albright K. Westinghouse. No relation to the zillionaires, I checked. Sitting next to Jerry in my threadbare jeans and flannel shirt, my attire coordinating with the frayed and colorless wingback easy chair to which I'd been assigned.

A once renowned-and-revered but now retired-and-recycled piano man; a self-medicating pro who can still remember—if not execute—a few hot jazz licks and a bit of Chopin, and who still keeps a tattered tux and scuffed patent-leather shoes in the closet. For the odd work-related emergency once called a gig. The K is (or was) for Kool.

I assumed that Jerry must have briefed Liv on our psychological profiles. If only to prevent any unrealistic expectations regarding our potential for taking guidance in the systematic quieting of thought, commonly known as meditation. Otherwise, the poor girl was in for a surprise.

Liv took a handful of lavender-colored booklets from her pack and laid them down on the piano keys up in the treble register. Then she reached back in and brought out a miniature gong that hung by a string from a small stand and set it with an accompanying mallet on top of the piano. She shot us a shy tip-of-the-fingers wave that made her look about seven years old (that birthmark still puzzling me)—and Ponderosa East's first ever introductory class in group meditation was about to begin.

I nudged Jerry with my foot. He opened his eyes and sat up straighter in the recliner and sneezed into his hand and wiped it on his robe. The Reverend Mary Kreapy sat rocking in the Bentley, shaking her head and muttering hateful nothings to no one in particular. Cora Eaton raised her tee shirt to wipe the drool from her chins, exposing her left breast. Irma Stank swiped at the air.

Well, I thought. This should be interesting.

Liv smiled uncertainly. She took up the mallet and lightly struck the gong. No deep resonant boom to inspire feelings of peace and tranquility, but instead the tense staccato ping of a half-muted chime. Then she sat facing us on the piano bench—her back erect, legs crossed in full lotus position, wrists resting on her knees, thumbs and forefingers making a circle—the symbol of perfection—and closed her eyes.

She took in a deep breath and exhaled while chanting softly.
Om...
A short silence, followed by another breath.
Om...
Silence. Deep breath.
Om...

Once more for good measure.

Om...

Liv opened her eyes. A wide sleepy grin appeared, suggesting serenity, if not an altered state of higher consciousness. Only to be met by a room full of blank stares, suggesting indifference, if not an altered state of hostility.

Om is a mantra, Liv said, which is a word we say to get our minds focused and centered while meditating. The word *Om* has its roots in the ancient religious teachings of India. It consists of four syllables, she said. First ahh, then ooh, then mmm—followed by a silent syllable, signifying the deep silence of the Infinite. Liv repositioned her arms on her knees. Why don't we all try it together, she said.

Om... she chanted.

Alone.

The vibrational frequency of her voice produced the exact same pitch as before, I noticed, impressed with her tonal memory.

Om...

Again, alone.

Om...

Once more, all by her lonesome.

Liv conjured up a benevolent smile. Everything in nature is pulsating and vibrating, she said. Nothing is standing still. By chanting *Om*, we're resonating with the unifying sound of the universe, acknowledging our connection—symbolically and physically—to nature, and all other living things. Shall we give it a try? she said.

Deep breath, eyes closed.

Om...

Still no takers.

Om...

Nada.

Om...

Zip.

Okay, she said, opening her eyes. Maybe later, then. She cleared her throat.

Let me explain why it's good to meditate, she said, speaking slowly and deliberately now, as though for the benefit of children.

Everything we are aware of arises in our field of consciousness, she said, including our thoughts. And with our thoughts comes our sense of self. In fact, our sense of self is generated by our thoughts, the thought of *I* or *me* being the core thought that appears to think all the other ones. This illusion of being a continuous self results from the brain indexing through our memories to find a common thread whenever a thought occurs. And so, as our thoughts arise and fall away naturally, so does our sense of self.

Liv paused to gauge the group's reaction, as the deep silence of the Infinite lingered on in the rec room. Broken only by Jerry's steady wheezing through a deviated septum.

Liv dismissed the residents' apparent apathy with another attempt at a good-natured smile. When we engage in mindfulness meditation, she continued, we practice observing our thoughts—the good ones, the bad ones, and the neutral ones—without judging them or acting on them. And sometimes, if we remain still enough and just watch, our thoughts and our sense of self will vanish.

She scanned our faces, searching for some sign of encouragement. Acknowledgment. Life.

When we experience being conscious without a sense of self, Liv said, we discover that our thoughts do not define us. And that, in fact, we are much more than just our thoughts. She paused again. Is any of this ringing a bell with anyone? she said.

I looked around the room. Palpable disinterest. Steady wheezing. A lot of wall gazing. But no bell ringing.

Not what she was used to, I thought.

The state of mind we attain in meditation is also restorative, Liv asserted, a trace of impatience audible in her voice now. The relaxed state we achieve slows down the nervous system, she said. Giving our brain a rest from the constant internal chatter that keeps us distracted. And exhausted. Which is a *good* thing, she said. Undeniably good.

The residents stared off, unmoved.

Helping us to feel *better*, Liv said, a bit riled.

Healthier, she said.

Physically, she said.

And mentally, she said.

Liv glanced at her watch. Clearly frustrated. Doesn't anyone here ever feel distracted and tired? she said, annoyed. From all the incessant internal chatter? she said, pleading. Little beads of sweat were collecting on her forehead. Well, she said, frowning. *I* do. She closed her eyes and sat up straight and resumed her former meditative posture.

Om...
Om...
Om...
O—

Jesus Lord and Savior! the Reverend Mary Kreapy said. This bony bitch is busting our balls bad, Jerry.

Jerry, snoozing, his narcolepsy having saved him from Liv's little lecture, leaned left and farted.

You can say that again, Doctor Wisenheimer! Cora Eaton said.

That was totally inappropriate, Ike, Irma Stank said, swatting at the stench—real and imaginary.

Sounded appropriate to me, Roccanne said.

I waited for the dust to settle, then I looked at Liv.

And there you have it, I said.

Fair enough, Liv said, defiantly. She stiffened, then continued.

Consciousness is what enables us to be aware of our selves, she explained. As far as we can tell, without it we wouldn't know we exist. But no one knows what consciousness is, exactly. Or how it happens, or where it comes from. We know it's connected to the brain somehow. And we know that we have it by the attributes we can ascribe to it.

Apple boots? Jerry said, waking. What's apple boots? Ascribe to what?

To consciousness! the Reverend Mary Kreapy said. Pay attention, Doctor Wise-Ass.

Ike's a doctor, Irma said, giggling. A tall handsome one.

Not a short fat one, Roccanne said. Like Jerry. The eighth dwarf. Sleazy, we call him.

Liv trudged on, undeterred.

It has been said, she declared, that consciousness is like a mirror. And that our thoughts—our beliefs and hopes and dreams—are to consciousness what objects placed before a mirror are to the mirror itself. Merely reflections on the surface. Appearances. Transient. Insubstantial. Unreal.

As if on cue, we all cocked our heads to the right and gazed into the full-length mirror hanging on the wall behind Liv. She turned and saw our skepticism reflected in the glass.

See? she said, wide-eyed. Everything can be seen in the glass, but nothing actually exists there. Equally important is the fact that the mirror remains unaffected, unchanged by the contents observed in it. She ran her hand over the surface of the mirror. Anyone feel that? she said.

She thinks we're daft, Cora Eaton said.

Who's daft? Irma Stank said.

Well, Roccanne said. If we're being honest…

Honest? the Reverend Mary Kreapy said. Like that hog-humping hussy up there?

Liv began to blush.

And just like the mirror, she said, her birthmark turning a spectrum of colors, our consciousness is unaffected by the contents that arise within it. Unchanged by our thoughts and feelings.

Unaffected? the Reverend Mary Kreapy said, ripping off her bathing cap. Un-affect *this*, you tit-tonguing trollop!

Liv winced at the sight of the scars criss-crossing the Reverend Mary Kreapy's scalp.

But if we identify with consciousness, Liv argued, instead of with our thoughts—if we become the mirror, so to speak—then we are no longer subject to the limits and biases of our own thinking. We're free!

Whoa-hoa, free! Cora said, twirling her index finger in a tight circle at the side of her head.

Give this girl an appointment, Jerry, Roccanne said. Like, today.

This feather-brained floozy doesn't need an appointment! the Reverend Mary Kreapy said. The fickle flirt needs a good flogging.

Jerry began whistling the theme from *The Twilight Zone*.

Liv ranted on.

Good things don't make the mirror good, she insisted, her pace quickening. Nor do bad things make it bad, she said, her voice climbing with each word. It's the same with our thoughts and consciousness, she exclaimed, wringing her hands. The purpose of meditation is to see that our thoughts are like reflections in the glass. They have no corporeal reality. No power over us. Only the power that we grant them!

Well, jumping Jehoshaphat, the Reverend Mary Kreapy said. This devil-dogging diva has drunk the Kool-Aid, Jerry!

Every last drop of it, Roccanne said. By the sounds of it.

So there's none left for us, now? Irma said.

Jerry tapped me on the arm. Time for some Kool-Aid, he muttered. As in, aid from Kool.

I took his cue and addressed Liv. So, I said, it seems you're saying that meditation gives us a break from our deluded selves. Helps us see through the illusion of the self—the source of internal conflict—and live a more calm and peaceful and happy life.

Liv's face lit up like a Halloween pumpkin. Yes! she said, again avoiding my eyes. That's correct.

Cool it, Kool! the Reverend Mary Kreapy said. Don't encourage her. The skinny scrawny skank!

Where's a razor blade when you need one, Roccanne said.

Please! Liv said. No sharp objects! Let's all just close our eyes and watch our thoughts till they quiet down. Especially the violent ones. And then I'll start counting, and when I get up to ten, we'll all try and identify with consciousness and become the mirror. Ready?

We all looked around the room, then at each other.

Jerry farted. Whoops, he said.

Asshole! the Reverend Mary Kreapy said.

That's Doctor Asshole to you, Cora said.

Oh come on, everyone! Liv said, folding her arms over her chest. Pouting sullenly. Can't we just try it once?

Mother of God! the Reverend Mary Kreapy said. Jerry, can I go to the bathroom?

Of course you can, Jerry said.

On that salami-slurping slut up there?

Of course you can, Irma said.

Will meditation help my joints? Cora said. They're so stiff.

You're probably rolling them too tight, Roccanne said.

I glanced at Liv. Like herding wild elephants with a toothbrush, isn't it? I said.

Liv ignored me. Defeat showing in her eyes. Her face crinkled up and she started to whimper softly, fingertips trembling at her lips. She ran a shaky hand over her birthmark—all of us watching in anticipation—and then the dam broke.

Okay, then! she said. Don't become the mirror. I don't care. She socked the piano bench with her fist. I've got problems of my own to deal with, she said. Serious ones. And I think...I'll take...that appointment.

The very next day, Liv Fuller became a patient of Jerry's, and one week later she moved in and became a resident of Ponderosa East. Jerry gave her the spare room in the basement in return for her guiding us (just Jerry and me, at first) in three meditation sessions a day, with the emphasis on compassion and mindfulness training. Jerry did his best not to snooze and fart his way through them, and in a few days' time—just as he had predicted—the other residents became curious and joined in. Roccanne being the only holdout.

But apart from the group meditation sessions and her private therapy sessions with Jerry, Liv kept to herself. She took her meals alone in her room and engaged in minimal interaction with the others, but kept a good distance from me at all times. When I mentioned this to Jerry, he said he thought Liv might be dealing with some heavy stuff right now, and suggested I give her space and time to settle in. Adjust to the new living conditions at Ponderosa East.

Then one day, in the middle of a morning session Liv was leading—with all of us acting about as relaxed and compassionate and mindful as it gets here at Ponderosa East—Liv started talking about her past.

As I always say, she said, staring idly down at the piano bench, meditation is my medication.

No sultry rhythmic bounce this time, I noticed.

But sometimes, she said. It isn't enough.

We all opened our eyes and focused our compassion and mindfulness on Liv.

What do you mean, not enough? Jerry said.

Not strong enough, Liv said. No matter how hard I try, or how long I sit, my mind won't be still. Images surface continuously. Along with feelings of guilt and shame.

Hmm, Jerry said. Guilt and shame. Best keep the focus on meditation while we're assembled, Liv.

Blaming myself for my mother's actions, Liv said. For causing her to leave us. Thirty-five years ago. I was only seven.

Now Liv, Jerry said. This might not be the best time and place to talk about your—

Sometimes my mind gets creative, Liv said. Sometimes in a good way, but sometimes…

We sat waiting. Watching. Wondering. Jerry started wheezing.

Sometimes I can't even find the mirror, Liv said, let alone become it. She turned and looked at me—more like through me. I act on my thoughts, she said. Good and bad alike.

With Liv making eye contact with me for the first time, I felt compelled to respond. That's human nature, I said. We all act on our thoughts, at certain times.

Human nature, Liv said, shrugging. I recall the day I caught them together, she said. I had come home from school early, heard voices in the basement. Laughter. Then moaning. I snuck down the stairs and peeked around the corner…and there they were…on the piano bench. A bench like this one, she said. Doing it!

Liv, Jerry said. Maybe we should save this for a private session.

At my next piano lesson, Liv said, still staring at me, I confronted him. My teacher. Of course, he denied it. Told me it wasn't him. That it couldn't have been him. Then, when I started to cry, he got up and left.

Liv, Jerry said, I think that's enough.

That night, Liv said, after I went to bed, my mother and father had an argument.

Liv… How 'bout we get back to meditating, and later on we can—

Mom was crying. Dad yelling. Glass breaking. Shattering on the floor. Against the wall.

Liv, Jerry said. I must insist—

Mom left the next day, Liv said. And never returned. Six months later—in the garage—my father hanged himself.

This has gone past inappropriate, Jerry said. Liv. Please!

I found out where he lived, Liv said. My piano teacher. And one day I followed him to a bus stop. He stood waiting at the curb. Alone. Except for me, hiding behind him.

Liv! Jerry said. This is quite enough!

I waited for the bus to pull up, Liv said. And then I pushed him into the street and ran.

Everyone gasped.

Jerry wheezed.

Human nature, Liv said. She took a deep breath. Then closed her eyes. *Om...* she said.

ATTENTION!

RESIDENTS OF PONDEROSA EAST

TODAY IS FRIDAY, JULY 5, 2019

IF YOU HAVE TO BE SOMEWHERE *ELSE* TODAY

FRIDAY, JULY 5, 2019

YOU'D BETTER TELL SOMEBODY IMMEDIATELY

CAUSE WE DON'T READ MINDS AROUND HERE

WE DON'T EVEN HAVE MINDS—SOME OF US

AND WHOEVER STOLE MY FUCKING EARBUDS

BETTER BRING THEM BACK TODAY!

FRIDAY, JULY 5, 2019!!!

Despite Liv's nightmare past and bold confession, she continued to lead us in our group meditation sessions three times a day. Little by little she started to come out of her shell, though not so much with me. Her story had had a dramatic impact on all of us, marking a kind of turning point in our individual consciousnesses. Even Roccanne was moved when she heard about it, and so joined our group meditation sessions.

A few weeks later, this post appeared on the walls of Ponderosa East:

TO MY FRIENDS AT PONDEROSA EAST
GOOD MORNING EVERYONE!!!
MAY MEDITATION BE OUR MEDICATION
TODAY IS MONDAY, JULY 29, 2019
PLEASE CHECK YOUR CALENDARS
IF ANYONE HAS AN APPOINTMENT TODAY
PLEASE LET US KNOW
SO WE CAN ACCOMMODATE YOU
HAVE A COMPASSIONATE AND MINDFUL DAY

As it turns out, we were all going through some kind of catharsis. A purging of our personal hang-ups and fears. Self-acquittal, Liv called it.

As if by magic—and defying all medical prognoses—the Reverend Mary Kreapy began curtailing the inappropriate language and insults in her speech patterns, catching and correcting herself on the fly. Even apologizing when something slipped out. Soon she wouldn't allow a single *damn it* or an *oh shit* out of anyone's mouth. Jerry came inside one day soaked in sweat and complained that it was *hotter than hell* outside. Why, Doctor Weisberg, the Reverend Mary Kreapy said. Inside the walls of this house—except when quoting from the Bible—I must insist you call it Hades. Hotter than Hades. Please, doctor.

Cora Eaton began working out at the Y and letting the hair grow out on the back of her head. She cut her bangs in front and cut out all the junk food she'd been living on and swore off the fast-food joints she'd been living in and began eating a balanced diet of fruits and vegetables, with a bit of fish now and then. Having lost forty pounds and two of her chins in less than a month's time, she bought new clothes. Jerry helped her update her resume and took her on a job interview and she began reviewing art exhibits for the *Providence Journal.*

After returning Roccanne's earbuds, Ike up and disappeared. Irma Stank claimed she sent him packing once she realized they weren't meant for each other. Due to the fact that he only existed in her imagination. Irma resumed her ballet lessons and fell in love with her instructor, Mister Rudy, a real person. Now she only wears her tutu in dance class.

Roccanne's attitude wasn't the only thing that did a solid 180. She added John Coltrane's "Naima" and Samuel Barber's "Adagio for Strings" to her play list, and finally dug out all that dirt and grime collecting under her fingernails for god knows how long.

Psycho-jazz-guitar-apist Jerry "Django" Jazz-berg managed to curb his flatulence and improve his hygiene and jazz playing enough to begin sitting in with the high school kids across the street at their jazz band rehearsals. Next stop, jam sessions at the Community College. Then it's off to the big time: A steady full-time jazz gig right here in the rec room of Ponderosa East. Making it the only steady full-time jazz gig in the known universe.

And as for me, Albright K. Westinghouse, the K once again stands for Kool, since I've been clean and sober now for twenty-one straight days. Which I admit has presented some unexpected challenges. Images of places I've been and things I've done have been popping up. Just fragments so far, the occasional flashback. Jerry has me rubbing capsaicin ointment on my hands to relieve the arthritis pain, and now I'm back to practicing my etudes and getting my hot licks up to tempo. Where they'll need to be when I join Jerry on the bandstand in the rec room at Ponderosa East. We've been rehearsing an old arrangement I wrote of the Hoagy Carmichael classic, "Stardust." Nothing not to love about that old evergreen...

> *Sometimes I wonder how I spend*
> *The lonely nights*
> *Dreaming of a song*
> *The melody*
> *Haunts my reverie*
> *And I am once again with you...*

Meditation, it seems, is a lot like playing a musical instrument: With practice comes improvement. The difference being, with meditation, the instrument is your mind. Throw in free room and board and some good coaching, and the improvement you make can change your life.

See, kids? Simple as that.

I began to wonder how long it would last.

One night while Liv was leading us in our group meditation exercises, she began telling the story again about her mother and the piano teacher. This time she held her gaze steadily on me from the beginning while she spoke. And when she came to the point where she confronted the teacher at her next lesson, her face crinkled up and got dark, and again the dam broke. Tears brought her to the floor.

I sat frozen on my meditation mat, watching Liv cry. Her anguish was heartbreaking. Everyone was staring at me now. Even Jerry was looking askance.

What are you doing, Liv? I said. I turned and faced the group. Who are you guys looking at? I said. Do you think that I had anything to do with this? Me? Having sex with Liv's mother? A married woman? Can you imagine me doing a thing like that? I can't. I know we're all crazy around here, but this is madness.

Well, you'd better not have done it, Kool, the Reverend Mary Kreapy threatened. That would be an unforgivable sin.

We don't think it was you, Cora Eaton said, eyeing me. But like you say, we're all crazy around here. We certainly hope it wasn't you.

I've hoped for things before, Irma Stank said. It doesn't work.

Hope's a heartless hairy-humped whore, Roccanne said. She looked at Jerry. I'm just quoting Mary, she said. Back when.

Jerry looked at me. What about your blackouts? he said. Years ago. Back when you were teaching. He glanced at Liv. Middle school kids, weren't they?

What the hell, Jerry! I said. Blackouts or no, I think I'd remember having an affair with a student's mother. And being pushed in front of a bus? That might spark some recollection, too.

There'd be an accident report, Cora said. We can check.

Hospital records, Roccanne said. We'll check them, too.

Newspaper articles, Irma said.

But not if the bus wasn't moving when she pushed him in front of it! the Reverend Mary Kreapy said.

Or if it was moving slow, Cora said.

Whatever! I said. This is preposterous.

Liv sat up suddenly and pulled her hair back. Do you remember this, at least? she said.

I studied the side of her face, hoping it would spark a memory. Make the horror real. A birthmark? I said. Why should I remember a birthmark?

Because, Mr. Westinghouse. You were the piano teacher!

I recoiled in revulsion. Swallowed involuntarily. I squeezed my eyes shut and tried to remember. Something. Anything.

It's possible, Cora said.

Anything's possible, Roccanne said.

Let's do the math, then! the Reverend Mary Kreapy said.

Right, Jerry said. Liv claims that Kool gave her piano lessons when she was seven. If so, he had to be interacting with her mother. Scheduling lessons. Collecting payment—

You people are out of your minds! I said. I never screwed Liv's mother on a piano bench. Or anywhere else. I never even met the woman.

The math doesn't lie, Kool! the Reverend Mary Kreapy said. Unlike you. You muff-munching mother fucker.

Literally, Roccanne said.

And home wrecker! Liv said, opening a folder full of papers. Here's the evidence. Music from my lessons, she said, handing it to Jerry.

Jerry scanned the manuscript. "Stardust"? he said, holding up a single page. It's the arrangement we've been rehearsing.

Let me see that! I said, grabbing the music. I don't remember any of this, I said. Only that they never practiced!

You know what I could go for right now? Cora Eaton said. A Double Whopper with cheese. Who wants to join me?

We'd love to join you, Irma Stank said. But Ike likes Taco Bell.

They never practiced what I gave them! I said, half dazed. In their lessons. There was always some excuse.

71

It was you! Liv cried. You ruined my life.

No! I said.

Okay, who took my pocket knife? Roccanne said. And my earbuds? Was it you again, Irma?

I sat there stunned by what had become a full-blown reversal of all the progress the residents had made since they'd first started meditating. It was like stretching an elastic band and letting go—everyone had snapped back to their former pathological selves.

You have no proof, I said. It's all hearsay. It's Liv's word against…

I turned to Jerry. Besides, I said, shaking, I could never have done what she's accusing me of.

Jerry eyed me. And why not?

It's physically impossible, I said.

How so? he said.

I hid my eyes in my hands. Because, I said. I'm impotent. Have been my whole adult life.

The room fell quiet.

Hmm, Jerry said. The drugs. The drinking.

I nodded. The side effects started in high school, I said.

So Kool can't get it up, Cora said. Think I might've had that problem, too. At one point or another.

No big boy for the bad boy? the Reverend Mary Kreapy said.

It doesn't mean he didn't try to do it, Roccanne said, eyeing me.

Can you prove it? Jerry said to me.

The medical records will, I said. At Cranston General.

We'll look into it, Jerry said. Medical records don't lie.

Everyone shifted their gaze to Liv. She sat staring at the piano bench.

Why are you doing this, Liv? I said.

Medical records don't lie, Cora said.

Only liars lie, Roccanne said.

Liars like Liv Fuller! the Reverend Mary Kreapy said. You sausage-squeezing sow!

Ike lies like a rug, Irma said. Like wall-to-wall carpeting, actually.

My head was spinning. The pack was going after Liv now. Biting at her heels. She looked broken and alone, an abandoned middle schooler again. I wanted to hug her. Protect her.

I faced the group. Look at us! I said. We've gone from kindhearted, meditating truth-seekers to a paranoid mob. Jumping to conclusions about things we don't know for sure. How bout we cut each other a break? I said. Show some respect for our shared humanity?

It was the residents' turn to do the recoiling now, as the deep silence of the Infinite came roaring back into the rec room.

Roccanne handed Liv a box of tissues.

Liv dried her eyes and got ahold of herself. As you all know, she said, meditation is my medication. But it doesn't stop the memories. The images. Mother at the piano. Father in the garage. You, Mr. Westinghouse, at the bus stop. Only I can stop them, she said. By becoming the mirror.

Liv, I said. I honestly don't remember. You, your mother, the lessons. The bus. Maybe someday I will, I said. But for whatever it's worth, I'm sorry. I'll take my share of responsibility.

No one said a word.

Liv met my eyes. Thank you, Mr. Westinghouse, for the validation. Late as it is. I can forgive you now, she said. And stop blaming myself. My mother's actions may have been my problem, she said, but not my fault. Now they're her problems. Wherever she may be.

Everyone stared off in different directions.

Moments passed.

Impotence, Cora said. That's treatable, right Jerry?

Jerry leaned left and farted. Whoops, he said. All depends.

Om... Liv said.

Om... I said.

Om... We all said.

After breakfast the next day, Liv asked me to take a walk with her. We left Ponderosa East and headed down Park Avenue towards Reservoir. When we got to the corner, we stood watching the busy morning traffic speed by.

A city bus pulled sharply to the curb and stopped.

Consciousness is like a mirror, Liv said, eying me as the passengers departed. Our thoughts like objects placed before it, she said.

Here we go, I thought. Same old spiel. Spoken like she hadn't been saying it a few times a day for months now.

She nodded to the driver and waved the bus on.

Mere reflections on the surface, Liv said. With no power over us. Only the power we grant them.

As the bus pulled away, I stood trying desperately to recall the events in question from thirty-five years ago: Giving Liv piano lessons on "Stardust" at age seven; having sex with her mother on the piano bench; being shoved into the street in front of a bus.

But "Stardust"? I suddenly thought. For middle school kids? Who never practice? I'm not that naive. You start them off with "Chopsticks". If you're lucky they stumble their way up to "Farmer In The Dell". You save "Happy Birthday" for the real prodigies.

Forget "Stardust".

I looked at Liv. If there's anything up here, I said, pointing to my head, it's buried too deep.

Liv reached into her backpack and brought out a small photograph and handed it to me. My mother, Eileen, she said. And me. At the piano.

I held the picture up to my eyes and searched it for meaning. The piano—a blond spinet. Eileen—a hot blond. Liv—a cute kid, with a birthmark. That was my total takeaway.

You could have pushed me just then, I said. Into the bus. It wouldn't have surprised me, I said. Or disappointed me. Why didn't you?

Liv pressed the button on the pole to change the traffic light.

"Stardust", she said.

I must have looked as baffled as I felt. The song? I said.

The piano, Liv said. You can teach me. I promise to practice this time.

A Greyhound bus blew by us just as the light switched to yellow.

That's why you didn't push me? I said. You want piano lessons?

The light turned red and the traffic reared to a stop.

Liv took my arm. There will be other buses, Mr. Westinghouse.

We stepped into the street.

Let's walk, Liv said. Let's you and me just walk, and be the mirror.

WINDBORNE TALES

Good morning, sir. My name is Janis Joplin. I'm a reporter for the *Choctaw Sun-Advocate*, the daily newspaper down in Butler. Beautiful day, isn't it?

That it is. So far.

Those willow trees are so lovely, the way the branches hang over the brook and sway in the breeze like that.

That they are. So far.

And I must say, you're looking relaxed and comfortable. Sitting there on your porch, in that rocker. Under your bright red MAGA cap.

That I am.

So far?

So far as America got things what needs to be made great again, yes indeed. Like m' cap says.

Is that a bentwood rocker, sir?

Always was. Don't see no reason why it ain't still.

I have one at home. My favorite chair in the house.

What's that name a yours again? Sounds like I might a heared it somewheres.

Janis Joplin, sir. Like the singer. If I'd've been born a boy, it was going to be Scott. Like the piano man. My folks favored the musicians.

Ain't ringin no bells. Sorry.

I see you're not wearing a mask, sir. Have you been vaccinated?

For polio, you mean? Or the measles?

For the virus. COVID-19.

Oh, that there's a laugh. That why you got your face all covered up?

Well, I just wanted to be careful, in case you have concerns. Would you mind if I took it off, then? And just kept my distance?

We suit our own selfs in this here part of the state of Alabama, miss. Which I take it you ain't from.

No sir, this is my first trip up to Divided. Such a remote and rustic little hideaway you've got here. And such a curious name for a town.

That there name Divided come from back in Civil War times. Back when some was for it, and some against.

I see. Only about fifty of you living here now, as I understand.

Forty-seven we was, last count. A cottonmouth took the Pike twins last summer. Then Christmas come round and old lady Mouncey fell down her well. Lookin for Jesus, or so they s'pect.

Oh, how tragic. I hear the locals call themselves *Dividends?*

That they do. Them what gets the joke in it.

Interesting. I'm from Toxey, myself. Just south of Butler. We're a tiny place, too.

Yeah, I heared of it. Never been. You must a lost your bearins somewheres along the way. Bein this far aways from home.

Actually no, I intended to arrive today. But I'll admit, it took some doing getting up the mountain. Wouldn't take much to veer off that road and tumble into the canyon, the way that wind blows. So hard and relentless. My old VW barely made it.

That there mountain wind'll do that. Put the fear a God in you, she will. Them treacherous curves narrowin to near nothin don't help none, neither. Many a pilgrim's perished on the way up. Even more on the way down.

But the way the road opens up to this panoramic view you have here, sir, was worth every doubt that entered my mind. I've never seen such a big beautiful sky. The valley and lakes to the south. So scenic and picturesque. It simply can't be compared.

That it cain't. Wind and all. Like lookin at the far edge of civilization.

That it is! Ah, this is more like it now. I can see you better without the mask, too. It always fogs up my glasses.

And by golly you're a right good-lookin gal behind all that face coverin foolishness. Right good shape and build, too. Might as well show it off.

Thank you, sir. Can I assume you're familiar with the newspaper I represent? The *Sun-Advocate?*

You can assume whatever you want in this here world, but not none of it might be true. Best you keep that in mind.

Well then, can I ask you something else?

Askin's free. It's tellin'll cost ya. But go ahead, just long as we get to it fore m' asthma goes on the attack. Got one foot in the grave already between that there and this here failin heart.

I'm sorry to hear that.

So I'll need to get back to m' relaxin and m' rockin on m'porch here pretty soon. Like you been sayin.

I'll try to be quick, then. I'm doing an article for the newspaper on the attitudes and views of Choctaw county residents on the subjects of racial and gender equality and LGBTQ issues. I'm also interested in any comments you may have regarding the violent mob that stormed the nation's Capitol building in Washington, D.C. last week. Would you be willing to share your thoughts on any or all of these subjects for the good of the story?

Gimme them there letters you spun off once more.

LGBTQ?

Thems the ones. I heared of em. Is that there Q the one for queer?

Well sir, it could be for queer, or for questioning.

Questioning?

Such as when a person questions their gender. Or their sexual identity. Their sexual orientation.

Orient, you say? You mean like goin in for relations with them little Chinese gals? What gives you them happy endings and all?

Not really, no. These are people who question whether they're homosexual or lesbian or bisexual. Or even whether they're male or female.

You mean they cain't just tell by lookin?

Well sir, for some people it isn't quite that simple.

Tell me what ain't so simple bout reachin down and feelin round for it?

Some people feel that the typical gender constructs of male and female don't reflect who they are. These are the transgendered among us, which is what the T stands for in LGBTQ.

You sayin they ain't neither man nor woman?

Not exactly. Their self-identity doesn't conform to the conventional notions of male and female gender. Often the gender categories we use to identify ourselves and others is a trap. Such categories can be restrictive. So, to better grasp the idea of queer in regards to gender and sexual identity, we ask questions like: Where does straight stop and bisexual begin?

Where does bisexual stop and lesbian begin? Where does male stop and female begin?

Never heard a them questions before. How bout this one: Where does devilry stop and clean natural God-fearin livin begin?

And still others may feel that they're third gendered.

Third what?

Both male and female at once. Sir.

Good Lord! What's the letter for that one?

Well, I assume it would be the Q. Or possibly the T.

There you go assumin again. What'd I just tell you bout that?

But, anyway, that's when he or she may have gender characteristics of both sexes.

He or she, you say. Don't you mean *it*?

It, sir?

Maybe they oughta add a *I* to them letters. *I* for *it*. They's more like fishes and frogs than human people, ain't they?

Oh, they're human all right. The biological term for it is hermaphrodite.

Hmm. I was just about to ask it that there was the term.

It's a Greek term meaning—

I know, I know. Leave it to them Greeks to go stickin their private parts into everything. Even their own selfs.

Well, sir, plants and some animals and even humans can have sex organs of both genders. And you'd be surprised by who some of these people might turn out to be. Could be one of your own neighbors. Or your family.

All right! I heared enough. Help me out a this here rocker and we'll take this business inside. The wind up here's got special powers, you know. She can hear everythin what's spoke, indoors and out. We cain't never hide a word a what's said from her.

Well…okay. If you say so.

That old wind'll narrate a story out into the world, what's always listenin! Even now she's busy tellin this here tale. Next thing you know, folks all knows your business.

Yes, sir. Let me get the door for you.

Hold onto m' hand tight now, and guide me over to that there couch.

There you go, sir. Where would you like me to sit? Shall we observe the social distancing guidelines?

How bout right here next to me? So's I can see you good. You bein such a pretty thing and all.

This okay?

Little closer. So's I can hear you good, too.

All right?

Close as you want is fine. Remember, the wind'll be broadcastin our words soon as we say em. Best you choose em careful. Now, let's move on to them questions on race. Race ain't as messy as—

Oh, but it is, sir. Society is asking the same questions about race these days.

It is? What society would that one be?

Ours, sir.

Ain't heared nothin bout it from mine yet.

For instance, questions like: Where does white end and black begin?

I know some'd say the end of a rope for that one.

Another question might be: Do these categories reflect reality?

That's a easy one: Real as real gets.

Or you might ask, Are they artificial constructions? Why were they made? Who benefits from them? Who decides the determinate attributes? The answers suggest that categorizing race and gender and sexuality produces models that set people up to be winners and losers.

Well then, I'd have to say we needs them models. Folks is born to be winners or losers straight from the get go, ain't they? Them categories is just for keepin em in their proper place, is all. Now you best get out your notepad, girl, and make it a thick one. Cause I got plenty to say on this.

Okay, Mr. Gully. Could you start by stating your full name and age and occupation?

How'd you know my name's Gully? I ain't said it to you yet.

A good reporter does her research before she sets out, sir. Also, I saw it on your mailbox. And the front gate. And on your pickup's license plate.

Oh. So you really is a reporter? And not just tryin to romance me?

Sorry if I gave you the wrong impression, Mr. Gully. After a short bio, if you'll present your views on racial and gender equality, and your stance on the LGBTQ faction of society. And finally, on the recent riots in Washington.

And here I been thinkin you been cozyin up to me, and maybe we'd—

And please speak slowly and clearly, so we can get a good recording.

You recordin all this?

As soon as you say it's okay.

Don't see no recorder machine.

I'll just use my phone.

Got a tape recorder inside your telephone?

Soon as I press this little red dot, I do.

Well, I'll be.

Please go ahead then.

All right. Name-wise, it's Angus Gully. That's G, U, double L, Y. Age-wise, I'm a good four times yours, easy. Size-wise too, by the looks of you. Occupation-wise…well…let's see. I make m' livin as a high-wire trapeze artist in a travelin circus. Without no net.

Excuse me, sir, but that seems pretty daring. And dangerous. Especially for a gentleman four times my age. And with your health issues.

Ain't you a bit young to be callin anybody a bit old for doin anythin for a livin? And ain't that a touch a ageism I heared in your voice?

Sorry, Mr. Gully. I didn't mean to imply—

Far as my views on folks as equals goes, lemme just say this first off. Some people got ideas inside em runs so deep there's not no reachin em with no kind a change. Such folks be theys ideas their own selfs. Ain't no rootin theys ideas out of em. *Embetted* is the word. DNA style. Though I got no exact idea what them letters stands for, cept somethin what goes way down deep inside a you. And I happen to be one of them people. Don't matter what reasonable reasons there might be for the rightness of my ideas to be wrong; this here kerfuffle goes beyond what's right and reasonable. Reason and rightness ain't but dust on the road to us what holds our ideas close to heart. We's singleminded, like the animals. We's now just the way we's always been, and always gonna be. It's our God-given nature, granted by the Almighty Hisself. Unchangeable. Unreasonable. Unforgivable.

I think I follow what you're getting at, sir.

Good.

But could you elucidate a bit?

Sorry, I cain't do that. But I can spell it out in spades for you, instead. I'm as white a white man as they come, and proud as a peacock to be one. What some folks calls a old fashioned white supremacist racist male chauvinistic pig. Been a darn good one all my life, too. Top of the line.

That's interesting. I wouldn't have doubted that, but still—

What's more, if you ain't one your own self, I reckon you'd be disgusted and probably afraid a me, too. And you'd be spot on right to be.

Well, I'm not disgusted by you, Mr. Gully. Not yet, anyway. And you don't seem harmful.

But if you *was* one like me, then to our ways a thinkin—mine and yours—all them creatures from them other races didn't never need to be born.

What other races do you mean, sir?

Thems with any kinda different style of face, or nose, or eyes, or lips, or fanny. Or hair, or clothes, or speakin, or worshippin, or politikin. Or religious believin, or fun seekin, or sexual behavin. Specially your different skin colorin. Your blacks, your browns, your reds, your yellows. And all your mixed hues.

I'm beginning to see what you mean by disgusted. Sir.

Me and you'd be thinking this here world'd be a lot better off without any of em. Comin round and defilin our whiteness. Suckin at the tit of our white plenty till there's nothin left for us, what's white and belongs here. And what's more, us what's always been here, and ain't plannin on goin nowheres, neither.

Well sir, what would you propose to do about—

What theys all should do—me and you'd be thinkin—is quit takin up our white space. Our white jobs and our white air and water and services on these here white plots a earth, that ain't theirs to take it up from. And get their un-white selfs on back to whatever lands they come from.

Ah-ha. I see why you said I'd be afraid of you if I was—

And notice I ain't spoke the N word yet. That there one what causes all the trouble.

I'm almost afraid to ask about the women and the—

Far as the women folk goes, they's here for the same one thing they's always been here for: To serve at the pleasure of men. White men. So's we can keep the wheels of civilization a turnin and a grindin and a haulin. Like the Almighty Hisself says we's s'posed to do. And they's s'posed to do.

I see, the Almighty Himself. Meaning yet another white man?

And concernin them there freaks a nature you been describin usin them letters and whatnot, me and you'd see it like this: Nature's got all the freaks she needs without takin on that queer lot too, that QBLT'in crowd, what with all them normal freaks I just explained to you about. And this here's why we got to have our guns and keep em close by. Like that AR15 hangin loaded on the wall by the potbelly. Cause what me and you knows for sure, is that all them freaks'll be hatin on us for what we are. And with good reason, speakin a reason.

Dare I ask, sir, what that reason might be?

Cause we be hatin on them first. For what theys ain't!

Ah-huh. Wow. I think I've got all that. Thank you for…well…for your honesty. And for sharing your—

Be a good gal now and fetch me my inhaler off the table. Fore I suffocate from settin all these here things straight for you.

Yes, Mr. Gully. Is this the one?

And m' heart medicine, too, so's I don't bust a gut from all this jibber jabberin.

Here you go, sir.

Now you best get to printin up all what I told you for your story, and lemme get back to m' rockin and m' relaxin. Less you want to sneak off to the back room for somethin a little more—

Actually, I really do have to be going, Mr. Gully. But thank you for your time and your views. And sir, may I shake your hand?

You mean…like one white supremacist to another?

Well…

Why not, then.

Oh yes, and one more thing, sir. The rioters that stormed the Capitol—

Amateurs! Ever one of em.

Why do you say that?

84

You don't go stormin no fortified U.S. Capitol buildin and forget to take prisoners. How else you gonna make your escape?

You know, I hadn't thought of that. They didn't take hostages. Maybe they had enough help on the inside, and figured they wouldn't need any.

I blame the main man for that.

You mean the Almighty, sir?

Nope. That there orange-lookin one. The President. He shoulda give that crowd he riled up more stricter commands in that speech he made. Stead a speakin in all them code words what coulda be took either way. He's the one responsible. Couldn't be no more aggravatin to us what knows better.

Are you saying you agree with the impeachment, then?

I agree *somebody* shoulda knowed better. And sought out professional help.

For the President, sir?

No! For that there mob what was doin his biddin.

I see. Well. Speaking of pros, sir, would you happen to know where I can find a Mr. Boone Drye? He lives here in Divided somewhere. My research shows he's related to you.

Boone's m' half brother on m' ma's side. Got a place up the road. But don't be wastin your time tryin to talk sense to old Boone. He's a troubled soul. Dangerous as he is old and ugly. And more racist than me and you'd ever admit to bein.

Is it true he was a professional soldier? A mercenary?

You just watch yourself, girl. That little mask a yours ain't gonna protect you none up there. Not with old Boone. He's half virus his own self. Always spewin out all kinds a poison to them what ain't expectin it.

Would you happen to know his contact information, sir?

Good Lord! If you young-ins don't never learn nothin. As the wind is my witness, cain't say I ain't warned you.

Hello? Anybody home? Could someone call off these dogs, please? And these...roosters?

Hang on, I'm comin. Sorry to leave you out there in all that dust and dirt with them filthy beasts, Miss Joplin. I ain't fed em yet today, so they're probably thinkin you're breakfast.

Me, sir? Breakfast?

Best you come inside. Company's friendlier in here. Dirt's cleaner, too.

Thank you. I wasn't expecting such a spirited welcome.

Well, ordinarily I like to keep em hungry. So's they'll be better at guard doggin. And meaner at roosterin.

I appreciate your willingness to talk to me about your views on racial and gender equality, and the LGBTQ—

That bunch, yeah, I recall your message. And them riots up in D.C., too. M' baby brother Angus filled me in on all what you asked him about yesterday. Sounds like you got yourself a earful in return. Heared he even give you a extra letter for that there—what's it called, acronym?

Yes. It was a novel experience, I must say, Mr. Drye.

Well, visitin with Angus has been called worse. I s'pose it's all that stress from bein a overaged, overweight high-wire trapeze artist in a travelin circus. Without no net.

Yes sir, I gathered that.

Why don't you take a seat in that bentwood by the woodpile, where it ain't so drafty. Angus says you take a shine to them rockers. And keep a eye out for spiders.

Thank you. I will. No MAGA cap for you today, sir?

Nope. Gave mine to Angus when they was passin em out free at the mercantile. Case he loses one, he'll have the other. Looks better on him, anyways. Sides that, I ain't so sure this here nation was made all that great the first time they slung it together, never mind givin it another go. Specially if you count what them native Americans got to say about it. Which most folks don't.

I take it you're not a supporter of our president, then?

Our president's got nerve, I'll give him that. He'd be the kinda outlaw what kills his parents and then begs for mercy cause he's a orphan.

I agree, sir. Strong on nerve. As are his supporters. Many of whom are powerful politicians, now demanding that his critics back off for the sake of unifying the country.

Well, the only thing worse than that kinda thinkin, is that kinda timin.

How so?

Sounds like your basic politician logic, to me. Got double-dealin wrote all over it. Like somebody sayin, I just beat up my wife, now my kids want to report me, but I don't think it'd be good for family unity.

Seems a fair assessment. I see you're wearing a mask.

Doubled it up for the occasion. Like you did yours. Wouldn't want to infect you, what with me bein half virus and all. Accordin to Angus.

It sounds like Mr. Gully's made a full report. For the record, I get tested before and after each interview. There's a site over in Pennington. Another in Pushmataha.

Good. Cause Angus said you was fiddlin with his inhaler.

He asked me to hand it to him, yes.

Shook hands, too. Without no gloves.

We did. I asked him. He said—

One white supremacist to another.

That's how he put it.

Well, okay then. We'll de-mask our selfs. This way, them glasses a yours won't fog up your view none. And I'll get to enjoy mine better, too.

I appreciate that. Sir.

Angus goes huntin out there at that Pushmataha Plantation, you know. Sixteen thousand acres worth of managed wildlife habitat. Where you can *harvest a trophy animal* is how they put it. Ask me, it's just a fancy way a sayin come satisfy your need for dominance, by blowin the brains out a some poor defenseless creature. Or just woundin it, so it runs off and dies slower.

Shooting managed game isn't considered sport by everyone, sir.

It ain't nothin like takin out a hungry mountain lion, or facing off with a angry grizzly on a moonless night, I'll tell you that much. Long as they eat ever bit a what they kill, I s'pose it's rightful. I'm vegetarian, myself. Never did acquire no taste for meat. Nor for killin it, neither. Them there folks what shoots it for fun is more what I prefer huntin.

I imagine that would tend to make you the exception in these parts, Mr. Drye.

Like Angus likes to remind me. And like I like to remind him, plenty a folks see it my way. But most of em don't live in Divided. Or maybe they do, but they just ain't as noisy about it. We're like the Third World, Miss Joplin. Only closer. At least we ain't Mississippi. Now that we got electricity.

Yes, sir. Would you mind if I record the interview?

I insist. And I'll take a copy when you're done.

Certainly. I'll be happy to provide a written transcript as soon as—

I'd rather you email it to me straight away. Mp3 file'll do fine. And I'll want to approve all what parts you wind up printin in the article.

Of course. Please begin with your name, age and occupation, and then your views as we discussed. Ready?

Let her roll.

And…3…2…1…recording.

First off, the name's Boone Drye. But some folks calls me Bone. Goin for the humor in it, I s'pose. I'm named after the famous frontiersman, Daniel Boone. The greatest bear-killin, Indian-fightin, trail-blazin, wilderness-tamin white man ever to go pro. I'm older than dirt, by local standards. Still makin m' livin as a professional hell-raiser. Self-employed. Freelance style.

Anyways, I'm a straight white male of northern European descent. Like m' half brother, Angus, what already warned you about me bein a dangerous racist. Which I pretty much am.

But sir, you don't appear to be at all like—

Well, there's a little twist in the rope here. See, it's m' own race I'm racist against. Not them others. Though ever lot got its bad apples, what oughta be culled out and fed to the sows.

Excuse me, but can you clarify—

I know what you're thinkin. White guilt. *He's one of them.* Ain't so. I ain't done nothin my whole life to feel that kinda guilt over. Cept for cheatin on a test one time to get m' driver's license. Wrote the answers on m' arm, and like a dummy raised it up to ask a question. The drivin teacher told me don't worry boy we're all going to hell anyways, so cheatin here and there ain't gonna hurt your reward none. But it didn't get me no driver's license, neither.

Apart from that, I never owned no slaves and I don't go round actin superior to my fellow beins. Be they humans or animals. Or trees or plants or insects. Not even m' close relatives. Though my ancestors did, and certain kin of mine still do. They don't own no slaves, but only cause it ain't lawfully allowed nowadays. It don't make me proud to be they kin, but I don't feel no personal guilt for what they done with their lives, neither. All it ever done was make me racist against em.

But how did you come to be this way, Mr. Drye? Growing up in the midst of all that prejudice and bigotry. Like your brother. And yet, you turned out to be so different.

Never did get to the bottom of it. Me and Angus. Livin under the same roof. Same rules. Same mother's milk. Same girlfriend till we was fully growed. And then turnin out as opposite as we done.

It does seem to defy reason. But then, Mr. Gully said reason and rightness are meaningless to him. He said his views are God given in nature.

Well, could be his god had somethin to do with it, I couldn't say. If I had a god I believed in—which I don't—I'd be prayin for their souls.

Mr. Gully's, you mean?

And that god of his, what give him them views he holds so dear.

Do you think Mr. Gully prays for your soul?

Don't see no point to it. Angus believes in a god what believes the same as Angus. But I got my own views on what them two rascals oughta be takin into account, about them there views of theirs.

And what might your views be?

Well, when it comes to this here notion of equality and discriminatin against them what ain't your own kind, a lot of straight white males—and their straight white male gods—don't seem to realize that bein straight and white and male in a world already ruled by straight white men means that we straight white males automatically enjoy greater privilege and position and power, as far as opportunities for advancement goes. Compared to your non-whites, and your women, and your LGB types. And all their gods. It ain't what you call a level playing field. But of course, most straight white men like the un-levelness of it. So they can have the upper hand, and keep all the subordinates subordinatin.

Mr. Drye, I never would have expected you to say that.

On top a that, no matter how lowly a straight white man's privilege and position and power may be, it's gonna be higher than the privilege and position and power of your non-whites and your women and your LGBs. And this ain't white guilt talkin here; this is white reality. And ever other color reality.

Is it common knowledge that you feel this way, sir? Here, in Divided?

I guess it's always been out there, blowin in the wind, like Angus says. He told you what powers that there she-devil got to tell her tales, didn't he?

Eh, yes. I guess he did.

What makes it some sort a miracle I'm still breathin in and out after all this time.

Do you think the locals respect you too much to cause you harm?

More like fear me. Which is worse. You know the sayin: Fear brings the finger in closer round the trigger.

So that's why Mr. Gully says you're dangerous.

Concern for the underprivileged scares the bejesus out of em round here, Miss Joplin.

Around everywhere, I'm afraid, Mr. Drye.

But what most of em don't figure, is that all this concern certain white folks say they feel for the underprivileged just ain't possible. It sounds good to say it, but we whites cain't never share the feelins of the underprivileged firsthand; it cain't be done cause we're already white and privileged, so how can we know what it's like not to be? The best we can do is understand that we cain't never understand. And just keep on tryin.

That's some very enlightened thinking, sir.

Well, it ain't my original thinkin, of course. Other folks must a thought it through by now. I'm just agreein with it, and passin it on. And there's plenty more where that come from.

Would you care to elaborate further, then?

Be delighted. This human race of ours is just a whole lot a folks with hand-me-down type features that lets us tell one lot from the other. But all these here separate lots belongs to the same breed. We're all human people. And the differences ain't hardly there at all, though it might not look it to the eye. Such as your skin colors. But science'll tell you that ever one of us shares 99.99 percent of the same basic goop—and science ain't about to lie to you, or it ain't bein scientific no more. So, dividin us up into a handful of races depends purely on a individual's frame a mind—on what they like and don't like, believe and don't believe—and not on no actual proof. That is, accordin to *Scientific American,* of which there's a few decades' worth settin in that pile by the fish tank.

Yes, I'm aware that science refutes any biological basis for race. But race does seem to have a social meaning, which has been legally constructed.

Maybe so. But legal don't make it right. Or true. It just makes it legal.

But there *is* a popular view of race that recognizes natural, hereditary divisions among humans, reflected in our physical forms and identified by terms like Black and White and Asian. Claiming that a person's ancestors and skin color make them members of a genetically defined racial group, and that the connection between human facial features and racial status is fashioned by nature.

Well now, just ask yourself one simple thing: What lot would this here view be so popular with?

I imagine with folks who want to maintain their race's rank and station?

Meanin them what wants to preserve and protect their higher rank and station. And their dominance over others.

Yes.

Can you imagine a subordinate race what would want to preserve and protect their race's lower rank and station? What would want to maintain their sub-ordinance to others?

No.

Me neither.

But the view that race has a basis in biology is upheld even by the United States Congress. And the Supreme Court.

Ah, well, that lot's always seein what kind a law-makin mischief they can get away with. Includin that there name supreme. Before us regular folks catches on and blows up a buildin or two in protest. Empty ones, we hope.

It's quite shameful, Mr. Drye. I recently read where Congress still holds the term *racial group* to mean those whose identity is distinctive in terms of physical characteristics or biological descent!

See what I mean? They just ain't up on the latest scientific scoop. And by latest, I'm talkin the late 1800s. For more 'n a hundred years now, science's been sayin there ain't no evidence what proves race is biological. In fact, it's just the opposite. There ain't no genetic traits all Blacks got but non-Blacks don't got, for instance. Same with Whites and non-Whites. Your races ain't determined by your genes. You got more genetic differences *inside* each of your so-called Black and White races, than between em!

I understand, sir, that the Supreme Court ruled—I think the case was Saint Francis College versus Al-Khazraji—that an Arab could recover damages for *racial discrimination*. Demonstrating a continued reliance on blood as a metonym for race.

Goes up your backend a mile, don't it? But I'm glad to see you're doin your research. Me, too. I printed this here off the Internet just this mornin. How bout I read it aloud for the sake of the recordin?

Please do.

Here goes, and I quote.

"…*The notion that humankind can be divided along White, Black, and Yellow lines reveals the social rather than the scientific origin of race. The idea that there exist three races—Caucasoid, Negroid, and Mongoloid—is rooted in the European imagination of the Middle Ages, which encompassed only Europe, Africa, and the Near East. Nevertheless, the history of science has long been the history of failed efforts to justify these social beliefs. As one scholar notes, 'the nineteenth century was a period of exhaustive and—as it turned out—futile search for criteria to define and describe race differences…' "*

Interesting. Just as science has failed to justify the conventional social belief that heterosexuality is preordained for all, and therefore homosexuality must be a choice. Society at large still considers it a preference, rather than a viable category of sexuality arising from natural causes.

All you need to know, Miss Joplin, is if science cain't confirm it, chances are folks's made it up. Usin their own personal beliefs to justify it. Wait now, there's more.

"…*The genetic studies of the last few decades have only added more nails to the coffin of biological race. Evidence shows that those features usually coded to race, for example, stature, skin color, hair texture, and facial structure, do not correlate strongly with genetic variation.*"

So, what the evidence *really* shows, sir, is that people take pride in denying the evidence.

Ha! Good one! And here's another slam dunk.

"Referents of terms like Black, White, Asian, and Latino are social groups, not genetically distinct branches of humankind. The rejection of race in science is now almost complete…"

Nevertheless, Mr. Drye, the general population apparently embraces these superficial human traits as proof of the existence of bona fide racial profiles.

Then let's hope they take this here one personal.

"… Anyone who continues to believe in race as a physical attribute of individuals, despite the now commonplace disclaimers of biologists and geneticists, might as well also believe that Santa Claus, the Easter Bunny and the tooth fairy are real, and that the earth stands still while the sun moves…"

Now if that don't explain Angus. Why, just the other night I caught him puttin a tooth under his pillow and hopin for a quarter in the mornin.

Excuse me, sir, but we'll have to delete that last comment from the record.

Okay, okay. This here policy statement by the Triple A will be the last one, I promise. Not the Automobile Club, mind you. These folks is the American Anthropological Association.

"Race simply cannot be tested or proven scientifically. Anthropologists can find no clear racial boundaries to show where one 'racial' group stops and another begins. It is clear that human populations are not biologically distinct groups. The concept of 'race' has no validity in the human species."

Ordinarily, this'd be the end of it. But, like Angus says, Reason and rightness ain't but dust on the road to them what holds their ideas dear.

Then again, Mr. Drye, reducing scientific evidence—or in this case the lack of it—to dust on the road has terrible consequences for the truth.

Like all them deep felt ideas a his, I s'pose. But probably there ain't no reason out there what'll make any of us see the rightness of our own ideas to be wrong. Mine and yours included.

Well sir, this has been very illuminating. And informative. I'm sorry to have to stop now, but I have another appointment. I could come back tomorrow to finish up the interview, if you have time. I think your views on gender bias and LGBTQ issues and that maniacal mob that stormed the Capitol building will be important to present to our readers.

Fine, then. Have your people call my people and set it up.

Your people?

That there maniacal mob that stormed the Capitol? Them people.

Excuse me, sir?

Seems maybe you didn't take Angus' warnin too serious. Bout me bein a troubled soul? And dangerous?

Actually I did, but—

Spewin out all kinds a poison and such.

But...

But what?

What are you saying? That these aren't your real views? You sounded so convinced. So...informed.

We may be Third World round here, Miss Joplin, but we ain't dead.

I don't get it. Are you saying now that you support racism? Sexism? Those anarchists?

I support tellin the truth.

Meaning?

Meanin when I called up that there *Sun-Advocate* newspaper down in Butler, the editor told me the only Janis Joplin he ever heard of is some singer gal what died from too much drugs. A long time ago. So, unless you was recently raised from the dead—

Janis Joplin happens to be my real name!

Ah, but you ain't no real reporter from no newspaper down in Butler, now, are you?

I plan to write the article first, sir, and then submit it for publication. And now, I really must be going.

What? No handshake? One professional hell-raiser to another?

I shook Mr. Gully's hand because he frightened me. And disgusted me. As I expected he would. And, frankly, I'm infectious. I figured it might humble him, change his attitude if he caught the—

Infectious, you say? Thought you got tested fore and after each visit.

I never said what the results were.

Leadin us to figure they was negative.

Just as you led me to assume various untruths about you!

Angus warned you about assumin things, Miss Joplin. How do you know all what I told you ain't true, cept for them mob people bein mine? How do you know all what Angus told you *is* true? How do you know we ain't switched roles, or been bluffin you? How do you know we ain't heared all about you fore you come? Direct from the wind, what give you such a hard time gettin up here? What's been reportin on this here tale all along?

It doesn't matter now, Mr. Drye. In fact, I have the virus. And I'm asymptomatic. Seems you're not the only one spewing out all kinds of poison. Perhaps you should call Mr. Gully.

And tell him what?

That he and his god won't last long if he contracts this disease. Not in his condition. Tell him that my name will soon be changing. To Scott. And that the T stands for me. He'll understand.

You know, Miss Joplin—or Mister, or whoever or whatever it is you are—Angus and me had us a hunch about all this. So I'll just let you tell him your own self. He's been waitin on you outside. Probably listenin in at the window. Along with the wind, I s'pect, what's beginnin to howl now. Like them dogs. What's still hungry and waitin on their breakfast.

Are you threatening me, sir?

I don't need threats for what can be fixed without em.

Good bye, Mr. Drye.

Angus! Miss Joplin's fixin to leave. Anythin you want to say to her fore she blows away?

That I do, brother Boone! The wind out here's a ragin, Miss Joplin! She's blowin up a mad gale. Tellin a mad tale. And she don't take kindly to connivers!

See that, Miss Joplin? And you thought gettin up the mountain was hard.

Wait'll you try gettin down.

ADVENTURES IN JAZZ

When you've got chops to burn on the axe, son, and you've done all your im-
itating and all your assimilating, then it'll be time for innovating. Time to
start playing your own solos and not just your version of somebody else's. Not
everyone has what it takes to go beyond the status quo; most of us are lucky
to be halfway decent copycats. But you're different, Blue. You're a hardcore
jazz improviser, one who'll show us new ways to play someday. I just hope
I'm around to play my version of you once you start laying it down. Now go
do as your mom says and give that math homework another try.

This may sound smug of me to say—in a paradoxical sort of way—
but I have to respectfully disagree with the older jazz musicians in
town who claim I was a child prodigy. I admit it was uplifting to
hear them say it, since back then I was hoping they were right. But then
I found out about Mozart—studying Bach's manuscripts and astonishing
the world by composing a concerto for orchestra at five years old—and I
thought, now that's a prodigy. I didn't start composing until I was eight.
Late bloomer, I guess. But even at that age, all I turned out were these
little diatonic jazz ditties, that I wrote in my little manuscript book and
played on the piano. By myself. No orchestra within miles. My Irish setter the only living thing whimpering in appreciation.

Or maybe she just had to go out and pee.

Then I discovered Charlie Parker. The bar doesn't get any higher than
Bird. Gets his first sax at twelve. Practices eleven hours a day. By fifteen he's
a professional musician. Then he quits school, masters the sax, and invents
a style of improvised music played around the world called *bebop jazz.*

Another prodigy. Albeit one with a tragic ending. Like Mozart, but
with stronger drugs.

And that got me wondering. What is it with prodigies and tragedy? If
that's the price we have to pay, maybe we're better off being average. Or
below, even. But then I thought, when has tragedy ever spared the mediocre? I'll bet tragedy has visited more losers than it has winners. Created a

ton of them, too. So, no one is safe, really. Better to be a tragic somebody, I guess, than a tragic nobody.

It's true that the elders in town took me under their wing and let me join the musicians' union when I was an underaged fifteen-year-old, like Bird—local #198-457 of the American Federation of Musicians in Providence, Rhode Island—so that I could start gigging around "legally" with some of the better professional bands in the area. Being tall for my age and quiet enough not to be noticed for anything but my playing, they figured no one would object.

It also helped—again, paradoxically—that my main instrument at the time was not the piano but the trombone, an instrument that had risen to prominence during the big band era of the 30s and 40s, and was still occasionally heard from while I was growing up in the 50s and 60s. And one that was generally considered to be super difficult to play jazz on. As true as that may be, to my mind it only qualified me as being sort of instrumentally challenged. More like a musical charity case than a wunderkind.

Our own young Blue Carson played the beastly and unruly slip horn with a steady solid beat and a driving yet buoyant swing feel, but all too quietly as compared with the ebullient high-energy phrases of the saxes and trumpets, as they detonated chorus after agile chorus... or so a critic wrote of my jazz playing at a high school jazz festival in 1966. Reading that review I couldn't help but wonder: Is it me? The horn? That ebullient critic?

Then my father—a well-read man and a semi-pro musician, himself—had this to say: *Ignore all non-playing jazz critics, Blue. They're like people who come out of their hiding places after a battle and stab the wounded. They are to art what shit is to food.*

I didn't quite know what to say to that.

It has been said that the trombone was invented by five people who never met each other. And if you compare the improvised jazz solos played on various other instruments by good players to those played on the trombone by equally good players, you'll hear what they're getting at. Or, just ask anyone who's tried to master the trombone, like Bird did the sax. Not that the sax isn't difficult too, but it's a lot more user friendly. And—like the trumpet and the guitar and the drums and even the piano—it packs a lot more projection power than *the beastly and unruly slip horn* when trying to be heard over the band during those roaring periods of high energy.

But what good is playing good, I thought, if it can't be heard good? (This was before I learned how to talk good.) And what do you do when—during those crowd-pleasing periods of high energy—your solo suddenly vanishes under the radar? Complain? To whom, the band? The audience? Your local jazz critic? Sure, you can lug around a microphone and an amplifier to provide the power you need at gigs and jam sessions and let the machines do the heavy lifting. But this was virtually unheard in the 1960s, and is snickered at to this day. Besides, far from enhancing the beauty of the natural acoustic sound of a musical instrument—which players spend years developing—amplification will certainly distort it, if not ruin it altogether.

Say, have you heard Blue Carson play lately? Of course you haven't, the pansy needs a mic and an amp just to be heard. And why bother? It sounds like a wildebeest giving birth over a public address system. Man up, Carson!

So why, then, did I choose the trombone in the first place? In fact, I didn't. Yes, I began life as a piano player, but in 1963 I just wanted to meet Louise DiBatista, the hottest girl in my eighth grade class at Hugh B. Bain Junior High School. Louise played piano in the school dance band, and I figured the best way to meet and impress her would be to get in the band. But since they already had a piano player (Louise), the only way to get in the band was to play an instrument the band needed. One—it turns out—that no one else wanted to play.

The band director nodded to the instrument case shaped like a trombone sitting by itself in the corner. I shrugged and walked over to it and drew my initials in the dust.

Am I crazy? I thought, hoping Louise would be worth it.

But, of course, by the time I was ready to join the band a few weeks later, Louise was already going steady with Chick Chichetti, the band's drummer. And a ninth grader. And a good ten inches taller than me. And Louise, too. But...a drummer.

That's what you get for letting your heart and your libido run your life.

So why didn't I just cut my losses and change instruments while I had the chance? Or simply quit the trombone and continue to impress (or depress) my dog with the piano? I've been asking myself those questions ever since. Blind loyalty is the only thing I can come up with. We Leos (my astrological sign) are nothing if not loyal to our commitments, as in, for better or worse, and, till death do us part. Which works fine, I guess, for things like marriage and going steady, but not so much for choosing a musical instrument.

Anyway, once I brought that dusty old trombone home and laid it in the tub and scoured it with soap and steel wool and totally destroyed the nice lacquer finish, and then played along with a few of my favorite jazz recordings, and then sat in with the band at my cousin Ethel's wedding a couple of weeks later, to the delight of my parents and relatives—we bonded. And the rest—with my dog howling away—is history.

What can you say? It's a basic law of nature: Drummers get the babes, tromboners get the blues.

But as a career-minded jazz musician, you can't beat it when your musical training begins on piano. The instrument cultivates in you a deep aural grasp of the relationship between melody and harmony, meaning you will more likely be able to play music by ear as well as by eye, which is the advantage most coveted by jazz improvisers.

My musical ear got so good from playing the piano every day that I could tell with my eyes closed which note was which, just by hearing it. Walking down the street I could identify the tones of car horns like they were letters on a sign. The ice cream truck's song, I discovered, was pitched in the key of B flat major. Our doorbell chimed the tones G sharp then E, unlike my grandmother's, which were G natural then E flat. One time at Christmas I even recognized the musical pitch of a fart! It was a D below middle C that ripped out of my Uncle Herman while he was rocking in a chair by the piano and eating dried fruits and nuts.

Now that's a good ear.

Another big advantage I had early on was that my father was a stride and boogie-woogie style piano player, whose love and enthusiasm for jazz may have eclipsed his instrumental skills, but never his dedication to the music. Dad named me after the famous jazz trumpet player, Richard Allen "Blue" Mitchell, one of his favorites. Dad would hold regular jam sessions in the living room, where my mother and all the neighbors would gather to listen and sing and dance, and I would get to play along with the band, unable to keep track of all the calls I heard for *Yeah Blue! Blow that horn, buddy! Louder! Faster! Higher!*

Dad would play recordings of Armstrong and Ellington and Tatum and Basie and Parker and Gillespie and Monk and Miles and all our heroes every morning before leaving for work, and every night till long after my bedtime. So, right from the start I heard how the true African-American art form of jazz was supposed to sound, and also how it evolved over the years.

Combine that with weekly music lessons from the local jazz giants, frequent high-end playing opportunities organized by my father (who would drag me out of bed to go sit in with whatever famous jazz star was passing through town), and hours of daily practice guided by mother (who patiently taught me the fail-safe divide-and-conquer method for improving my musical weaknesses—*Remember, Blue, as we practice, so do we play*), and almost nightly earfuls of encouragement and constructive criticism from the neighbors—and it's no wonder I was making decent progress.

Still, compared to the best young jazz players I heard at the National Stage Band camps each summer, and in the All-State Youth Jazz Bands throughout the region, I may have been younger, but certainly no better. And in many cases, not as good. Especially when it came to *detonating chorus after agile chorus*, full of *ebullient high-energy phrases,* on the *beastly and unruly slip horn.*

With the crowd screaming, *Louder! Faster! Higher!*

I graduated from high school thanks to a deal I made with the school's band director, Clement Burns. Otherwise, I'd probably still be there.

Mr. Burns caught me hiding out in the band room one day, practicing.

Blue Carson, he said. Where are you supposed to be right now?

I laid the horn in my lap. Math, I said.

Chuli's class? he said.

I nodded.

He eyed me. Here's the deal, Blue, he said. You play in the school concert band and the marching band and the jazz band for me, and I'll sign two cut slips per week for you. Provided you hunker down in math and English, and only skip classes to come down here and practice.

I looked at my horn, the lacquer still gone, and found a new dent. But those bands really suck, Mr. Burns. And I will too, if I don't practice.

Take it or leave it, Blue, he said.

Five cut slips, I countered.

Three.

Four. And I'll give English a shot.

What about math?

Forget it, I said. I'm hopeless. Mr. Chuli hates my guts.

Done, Mr. Burns said, shaking his head along with my hand. I'll do what I can about Chuli, he said. I'll probably have to play his kid's wedding for this.

But the more my jazz playing improved as a result of our deal, the more I realized how much further it had to go. And that there was no end to how much better you could get at playing jazz, if you practiced. It seemed to be one of those questions that was never meant to be answered—just asked. And if there was anything truly prodigious about me, it was my work ethic when it came to practicing. Born of my ambition to experience playing jazz at the highest level humanly possible. The level of my heroes.

I began to see that the only way to control my obsession for improving was to keep my agreement with Mr. Burns, and somehow learn to be satisfied with my dissatisfaction. As long as I could hear my playing getting a little better each day—meaning louder, faster and higher—I'd find a way to bear it.

I began my first year of college as a junior at Berklee College of Music in Boston. And at the end of my second semester, I got an offer to play in the trombone section of a world-renowned fifteen-piece jazz big band led by soprano saxophonist Cootie Verman. Cootie—a short balding man in his late 50s, with eyebrows like jungles and nostrils that flared—had already won a few Grammys and was a fairly major jazz celebrity. And, as I would soon discover, a much better celebrity than he was a musician. Or a bandleader. Or a human being.

But all I cared about initially was that his band was full of terrific jazz players, many of whom were already heroes of mine. And also that, for the better part of my existence, I'd dreamed of living the unabridged life of a full-time professional jazz musician. And here was my chance.

So, in the late spring of 1969, I decided to take a leave of absence from school and see the world through the smoke-stained windows of a rented Greyhound bus. With faulty AC, sticky floors, one toilet, a double window seat all to myself at the rear of the coach—decent enough for practicing, provided I used a whisper mute and aimed my trombone slide into the aisle—and thirteen other like-minded souls (since Cootie either flew first class or took a limo) whose singular passion in life was playing jazz.

Well, in their case, a double passion: Playing jazz, and getting high.

At eighteen, I was the youngest member of the all-male band (women still being shunned for their innate superiority), and the least experienced—musically and narcotically, and likely in other areas as well. I had never done hard drugs. Hadn't even smoked pot. I wasn't against doing drugs, just not interested in them for myself. Too busy practicing and playing.

At this point, I was still naive enough to believe the trumpet player who sat across from me on the band bus—a handsome playboy type and a major league jazz player in his mid 20s named Henry Hart, one of several African-American star players on the band—when he told me he was diabetic and asked me to tie his tourniquet before the gig each night so he could inject himself with insulin. Henry chuckled when I looked at him seriously and said, Sure, I'll tie you up. But remember, I'm not a doctor.

Immediately, Henry started calling me Little Lord, short for Little Lord Fauntleroy, and the name stuck. Everyone started using it, even Cootie. It was cool to have a nickname, even though I knew they were saying it to mock my naïveté. I'd been mocked before by lesser betters than these. And each night before the gig, Henry would extend his arm and fire off a wink and a smile and say, Hey Little Lord—time to tie me up!

I'd never seen a reaction to insulin like the one Henry had every night, which was starting to make me suspicious. But then I'd never seen a reaction to insulin period, so how could I have known the joke was on me? That is, until Henry used a contaminated needle and woke up yellow one day. We dropped him at an emergency room somewhere in Wichita, and a week later he was back on the band. His complexion still sallow, his arm still swollen, his jazz playing still burning up everything in sight.

There were more than a few hardcore junkies on the band when I signed on, and by the third week of the tour I learned that they were holding a contest to see who could be the first one to get me high. Each made valiant efforts, including six-foot-six Gopher Haze, the band's road manager and a former professional body builder from Detroit, who spoke with a thick German accent.

Zis ist ze goot stuff, Liddle Lawd. Vat God hizelv zmokes ven he vanz to got high unt dig zom kool jass unt hung out vid ze ladiz!

They were all trying to convince me of the merits of using. Promising deep musical insights into the esoteric dimensions of jazz improvisation.

Well okay, I thought, maybe they do play better than I do. But how do they know it's due to the drugs? Look at all the terrific jazz players who don't use (at least you wouldn't think they do). And look at all the troubled souls—like Bird and others—who did. And do.

One day we were on a thirteen-hour bus ride to our next one-nighter, and I said to Henry, You claim drugs give you deep insights into playing jazz. Don't you mean into self-loathing?

Henry smirked. Try self-forgetting, he said, lighting up a joint. We do it to forget.

To forget? I said. As in, escape? To flee reality, like a coward flees a battle?

Henry exhaled a squall of smoke. And what reality would that be, Little Lord? You think yours is the only one out there?

I didn't know what to say to that.

I'm talking about fleeing the constraints of the self, Henry said. To disappear into the music. Become the notes. Undivided by thought. That's not fleeing the battle like a coward, that's living the battle. Takes nerve to go there, man. Guts. You have no idea.

Henry turned away and went back to reading his little green book.

What's that book you're always reading? I said.

I don't think you'd like it, Henry said. It's about…ultimate reality.

I shrugged as I unsheathed my trombone slide. I didn't know what to say to that either, so I sat there and cleaned my horn. I wiped the inner slide dry and put a dab of lubricant on each length of tubing and rubbed it in with my hand until the heat from the friction melted the cream onto the metal, coating each tube with a slick slippery sheen. Then I sprayed the inner slide with mist from a water bottle and inserted it back into the outer slide and worked it until it flew back and forth effortlessly. Satisfied with its condition, I packed it up and then peeked over at Henry, still reading intently.

Hey Henry? I said.

He didn't answer.

I want to understand what you said a minute ago.

Don't worry, Henry said. You will. In time. Or maybe not. He scoffed. Either way, it's nothing you're not already doing to some degree. Sometimes. Maybe. Without the pharmacological escort.

But curiosity soon got the better of me—or maybe it was my own self-loathing—and one night before the gig, I caved. My roomie, the bass trombonist Tommy Trubbel—a stubby African-American cherub looka-like, about as wide as he was tall—claimed victory and took first prize: A Maxwell House coffee can full of Mexican weed laced with mescaline—which is what was in the joint Tommy used to cop my cherry. Supplied by none other than Henry Hart, who insisted on being credited with an assist, entitling him to a share of the spoils.

Being high for the first time on such a potent package, I didn't know what to say or think. For about two days. All I remember saying is how empty and clear my mind felt while playing that night. And how my solos seemed to play themselves, with me being more of a silent observer than the usual control freak. To which Henry responded, Not bad—for a first time escapee.

I was stoked by the revelation. But also wary of it. It felt like I'd been introduced to something as potentially dangerous and destructive as it was insightful and meaningful. Something that required an exchange. A this for that. Something that came with a price.

Something that would ultimately involve a choice.

The turnover for players on the Cootie Verman Big Band was highest for the chairs not held by junkies, which surprised me until I learned the reason why. The addicts—with ages ranging from the mid-twenties to mid-fif-ties—were easily the best jazz players in the band, and had been on the band for the longest time as well, some for a decade or more. Some didn't even have to read the music, not for any of the hundred plus arrangements in the band's library. And if somehow they forgot how their part went, they'd make one up on the spot that sounded better than the original.

But the reason the addicts stayed with the band—instead of using it as a stepping stone to move on to better (if not bigger) things—was much less impressive.

They would use up all the dope they had at the ready—everything from cough syrup with codeine to heroine mixed with cocaine (a potentially deadly favorite)—and then borrow against their salary to buy more. Eventually they'd get strung out and have to go into rehab, after which they'd have to rejoin the band to pay off their debt. Invariably, they'd start using again.

It was a classic vicious circle, and one that Cootie Verman himself helped to perpetuate by lending money to these brilliant but desperate players. In order to keep them on his band.

One night after the gig, Cootie caught me heading for the bus and pulled me aside.

Great playing tonight, kid, he said. You got all these bastards worried.

I felt a question mark form on my face.

Especially Henry, Cootie said, following up with a devious chuckle. By the way, he said, Henry says your playing sucks, you know. You don't play loud enough. Fast enough. High enough. All the shit the crowd goes nuts for.

I didn't know what to say to that.

So, what're you gonna do about it? Cootie said. I'd bury Henry Hart if I were you, next time you're at the mic. Show him who's better. Who's boss.

I looked him in the eye. Sorry, Cootie, I said. I play the solo as I hear it.

Cootie blanched. Then he eyed me hard. Well, you better *hear* how to prove Henry wrong, kid. Cause if you don't, I'll get somebody who will.

I held the old coot's gaze, trying not to smirk at those eyebrows-a-groping, those nostrils-a-flaring.

Why do you egg them on? I said. They get so wasted they can barely stand up and play, and then you bet money on them, like they're roosters in a cock fight. They're strung-out human beings, I said. They're hurting, and making you rich and successful in the process. They deserve your respect.

Cootie grabbed my arm and squeezed. They're junkies! he shot back. They crave attention. And approval. Mine! They want to win. Be the best. Betting on them makes them go for it. And that's good for them, and for business. Cootie poked his finger at my chest three times. Louder, faster, higher, he said.

As soon as I got on the bus I brought it to Henry.

It's true, Little Lord, he said. You got a lot to learn. Who doesn't? But I never said you suck. Cootie tells me the same shit. That you badmouth me to everyone. That you're a jealous punk who needs to get his jazz ass kicked.

Henry, I said, I never once said—

I know, Henry said. That's just Cootie, stirring things up. Pissing us off so we'll try to outplay each other on the gig. Get the crowd going, and yah-diddi yah-diddi. He does it to everybody who can play.

That demented slug of a human being, I said.

Just ignore him, Blue. And keep playing your ass off like you're doing.

I can't just ignore someone who pulls that shit, Henry.

What else you gonna do? Henry spit back. Quit? Then he wins anyway.

Henry said the word quit like it was a virtual impossibility. Like we'd all already made our beds, burned our bridges, and it just wasn't an option.

And I thought, maybe for him, at this point, it really wasn't.

It was general knowledge that Cootie Verman had made some bad business decisions that cost him large sums of money, and caused him serious problems with the IRS, which had made him bitter and cynical. Still, to my mind, that was no excuse for the way he treated *his* players, as he called them. Whose jazz playing was the only reason *his* band was still working and winning awards, which enabled *him* to pay off *his* debts. But worst of all, it seemed as though *his* players had stopped caring about being taken advantage of by *their* boss—because their boss happened to also be their source. And a pseudo father figure.

You'd find yourself in a hotel lobby or in an elevator, alone with Cootie, and you'd say a courteous hello. And he would ignore you. Turn his back on you and act like you weren't there. Or like he had no idea who you were. As if you hadn't been sharing the same stage with him and wincing at his syrupy slick cliche jazz licks every night for however long it had been.

One time I got so annoyed with his attitude that I stepped out of character (slightly) and spray painted over his name on the front of one of the music stands, changing the spelling from V-E-R-M-A-N to V-E-R-M-*I*-N.

After the gig, Cootie stomped onto the bus (the only time he visited in the four months I was on the band) and screamed that we were all fired unless someone owned up.

When no one gave me up, Cootie held up a hundred dollar bill—which in 1969 would've bought a healthy dose of your drug of choice. All those druggies sat licking their lips, but no one said a word.

Then Cootie tried to sweeten the pot—so to speak—by promising extra solo choruses (normally limited to one chorus per player, per song). No takers. Then he offered extra solos (normally limited to two or three solos per set, per player). Nada.

Cootie stormed off the bus and sent Gopher Haze to tell us that—Kooti sez zere vill be no pay checkz, unt no drawz, unt no handz out, until ze moozik stand ist vixed unt ze guilti pahti convezzez.

Poor Gopher had to deliver the bad news to Cootie in his limo.

Everyone turned to me and shot me a thumbs up. I hid a self-satisfied grin and reached under my seat for the paint remover. As I did, Henry Hart leaned across the aisle and handed me a piece of paper on which he had divided $100.00 by 13, making it clear that I owed each band member $7.69 for not ratting me out.

Maybe they still cared after all, I thought.

Our next gig was at a mafia-owned supper-slash-strip club in Detroit called the Pussy Cat Palace. The club was run by two brothers, Bobo and Sluggo Morrello, whose lives Gopher had supposedly saved during World War II.

We were about to go on for our last set of the night, and Cootie and Gopher were at the bar chatting. I was standing a few feet away, nursing a Coke and enjoying the opportunity to ignore Cootie off the bandstand.

I watched Tommy Trubbel sidle up next to them.

Buy you a drink, Cootie? Tommy said.

Stone-faced, Cootie nodded. To the bartender, not to Tommy.

When the drink arrived, Tommy said, Say Cootie, I'd be glad to hand-copy all those unreadable instrumental parts from the older arrangements in the band book, if you'd like. So the new players can read the music easier.

Cootie stood studying his drink. Then he said, Fuck the new players. They're more—he paused—*trouble* than they're worth.

Being a new player himself, Tommy tried for a smile but couldn't pull it off. I don't want any money for it, he said, apologetically. All I'd like is a chance to play a solo now and then. Just a short one, if that's okay. Blue said I could play one of his.

Cootie stalled for effect, then he shook his head in mock disbelief. Then he downed his drink and turned to Gopher, and with an icy stare aimed at Tommy, he held up two fingers and walked away. A not-so-subtle message: Two weeks' notice to Tommy Trubbel—for being a new player, *and more trouble than he's worth.*

The word got out before we hit the bandstand (I swear to God it was me who spread it) and the entire band mutinied. They refused to play a single note unless Cootie hired Tommy back.

There was a standoff for about twenty minutes, and the crowd was starting to grumble and tap their drinking glasses with the silverware. Finally, Cootie and Gopher were invited into the office where—according to Gopher:

Sluggo—ze loud scary one—tellz Kooti to zit down. Unt zen Bobo—ze quiet scary one—tapz ze bazeball bat on ze hand unt explainz ze obffious until Kooti gotz religion.

The band played its drug-infested heart out during the final set that night, swinging with a kind of all-for-one and one-for-all solidarity I'd not heard it do before. And old Cootie looked like he was about to implode when Tommy Trubbel approached the mic and took my solo spot on a tune Henry Hart had composed for Gopher Haze called "Bluez Vor Vinnez Unt Loosez".

At the end of the night, the crowd rewarded us with a standing O, and Cootie couldn't wait to beat it the hell out of there.

Our bus driver was a stick-thin elderly African-American gentleman, with snow white hair, the occasional tooth, and eyes that never stopped smiling, named Spoon Wilson. I addressed him as Mr. Wilson out of respect, and he returned it by addressing me as Mr. Fauntleroy. Spoon Wilson was a self-professed full-time alcoholic and troublemaker, and had been the band's driver for many years. The only thing he loved more than jazz was (or is it *were?*) the musicians who played it. But being a professional troublemaker, he would fall off the wagon fairly regularly, and when he did, the management would send in a substitute driver.

On one such occasion, the sub was a defrocked Pentecostal minister from Louisville named Millard Whipple—who lived on Kentucky Fried Chicken and diet Coke, and went barefoot on the bus and wore his pants high up around his midriff. Turns out old Millard strongly disapproved of the band's lifestyle. You'd have thought the Christian radio station playing nonstop in his ear buds—and the King James Bible open on the dashboard to punitive passages from the Old Testament—would have told us something.

On the fifth night of Millard's employment, we'd just finished up a two-night stand in Albuquerque and set off for our next scheduled hit in Chicago, a mere twenty-one hours away. It was Henry's turn to tell the band its nightly off-color bedtime story, and so he stood in the front of the bus with the driver's intercom mic to his lips, and held court.

One day the circus came to town, Henry said. *And everyone hurried off to see it. But on opening night, the lion tamer was attacked and eaten by a ferocious lion. So the circus owner, being desperate, ran an ad in the newspaper for a new lion tamer. Two people showed up for the interview.*

The first one was a beautiful voluptuous blond, named Suzy Biggabreast, and the second was a funny-looking barefooted guy with below average intelligence, named Millard Whipple.

Henry winked at Millard, who scoffed in disgust and kept driving. Henry pressed on.

The circus owner looks at the two applicants and says, Okay, who wants to go first? Suzy says, I will.

So Suzy opens the door and steps into the lion's cage and strips off all her clothes and starts dancing seductively in front of the lion. The lion roars and charges over and then snuggles up to Suzy and starts licking her all over her body.

How's that? Suzy says to the owner.

Impressed, the circus owner turns to Millard. Can you do that? he says.

And Millard says, Sure I can. Just get that lion out of there first!

Meager chuckles morphed into moans. Moans into groans. Groans into boos and hisses. So Henry slinked back to his seat while the band pelted him with plastic bottles and paper cups and food containers and used syringes. And then they all doped up for the long ride to Chicago.

Several hours later, rays of sunlight began seeping through the grit-encrusted window, warming my face and teasing me out of my unmedicated sleeplessness. I gazed outside and was surprised to see us parked across the street from the Kansas City, Missouri, Police Station.

Surprise turned to shock and shock to panic when I looked up front and saw Millard standing up and gathering his things. He was wearing shoes.

Hey! I shouted. What're you doing? Where're you going?

Millard took a few steps down the aisle and reached for his suitcase in the overhead rack.

Y'all are a pack o' heathens! he said. Goin' straight to hell, y'all are. But first, y'all are goin' straight to jail.

I started down the aisle. Stop him! I yelled. He's busting the band. Somebody stop him!

My screams rousted Gopher Haze, sitting in the row behind the driver's seat. Gopher stepped into the aisle and blocked Millard's escape, and the two of them started to tussle. Tommy Trubbel dove over his seat and grabbed Millard from behind and wrestled him down behind the first row of seats and sat on him to hold him there. Then Gopher reached down and held a pillow over Millard's mouth to muffle his cries for help.

Henry dashed past me and slipped between the seats and stomped on Millard's hand until he opened it and gave up the keys. Then Henry hopped into the driver's seat and started up the bus and pulled us out into the traffic.

Half an hour later we reached the outskirts of town and stopped to gas up. I jumped off first and found a pay phone so Gopher could call Cootie at his hotel suite in Chicago, and relay the news.

Vat ze fuk, Kooti! Gopher yelled. Zis muzza-fukka ist bat newz.

Cootie's response was that it wasn't his problem, and that it was time the band cleaned up its act. This—he said—while no doubt secretly hoping *his* players would remain *his* addicts so he could continue to extort *their* services for the sake of *his* professional and financial gain.

I say we beat the ever-living shit out of him right now, Tommy Trubbel said. Then drop him in a ditch somewhere.

You mean Millard? I said. Or Cootie?

Zat bazztid vanted to put ze scrooz to uz goot, Gopher said.

You mean Millard? I said, again. Or Cootie?

Then Henry chimed in. We should bring him to a barn, stick his dick in a vice, give him a dull spoon, and set the fucking barn on fire.

You mean Millard? I said. Or—

Yeah, Cootie too! Henry yelled. Why not? Fuck Cootie. There, you happy now, Blue?

Can I say something? I said. Let's get to Chicago and then let him go. Before we get there, everyone seals up their goodies in airtight plastic bags. We mark whose is whose and stash them in a storage unit somewhere. In a locker, with a padlock, at the Y. Somebody collects them later on, when the coast is clear.

Tommy grimaced. Later on? he said. Like, when later on?

Henry looked askance. And when has the coast ever been clear? he said.

Zounds zmaht, Gopher said. Vidout ze effidenz, itz hiz verd against ozz.

Case closed, I said. Liberty and freedom and intoxication for all.

But never threaten an addict with delayed gratification. And so, I can't say what ultimately became of Millard Whipple, because I really don't know. All I know is, they kept him tied up and gagged and shot full of dope for the rest of the trip to Chicago. Old Millard was one happy hostage by the time we got there, whether he knew it or not. And before the gig that night, Gopher made another call. To Detroit this time, is all I know. And after we finished playing and got back on the bus, Millard was gone.

Christ, I said. We're in deep shit now. How the hell'd he get away?

Tommy winked at me. Hmm, he said. Must've escaped. Houdini style.

Henry sighed. I just hope we never hear from that prick again.

Gopher shook his head. It voot be unnatural, he said. Zupa-dupa unnatural zat anyvon effa hearz from zat prick again.

I started to look for reasons to stay on the band. I could appreciate the bonding between the band members, united by their common habits and interests—mostly illegal—but at this point the gig was not helping me to evolve musically. The pressure was always on to play louder, faster and higher than everyone else, whereas I wanted to play my own solos instead of my version of theirs. And not while doing twenty years in the Missouri state pen.

The main reason I stayed on was to experience the highlight gig of the tour: Opening for the mega-famous rock band, The Who, at the Fillmore West Auditorium in San Francisco. It seemed like an unusual musical pairing to me, but this was California in the late 60s, so.

The Who was (or is it *were?*) promoting their new rock opera, *Tommy*, which featured violent displays of what had become known as *auto-destructive art*—an activity that involved the band members exploding their guitars by smashing them into various assembled drum kits and a row of six-foot high amplifiers that stretched across the entire back of the stage—as the climatic closing gesture of their performance.

I thought: You could feed and shelter more than a few homeless families for a long time with the money they spent on it during one performance alone. Wasted on it, I should say. *Or you could stay cooked forever on the best horse* (heroin) *this side of heaven,* as Henry lamented. Cootie was thrilled about the high-profile gig, citing all the press the band was getting (meaning that he was getting), and the huge payday it meant (meaning a huge payday for him).

One perk of the gig was getting to stay in a motel and sleep in a real bed again. Some of the guys on the band—*road rats*, they're called—were so used to sleeping upright on a bus that they would check into a room and find a chair to fall asleep in. I decided to spring for a private room this time, rather than ghost in someone else's room or take on a roomie to save on expenses. This was the first time I had splurged on accommodations since the tour began. And although I had another whole year of college to save up for, I was desperate for some peace and quiet and alone time. And also for enough room to use the full length of my trombone slide while practicing.

Standing backstage before the show, I gazed out from behind the curtain at a dangerously overcrowded auditorium. Through the dense cloud of smoke that engulfed the masses, I could make out people sitting or lying on what you had to assume was the floor, since you couldn't see it. Many of them went bare-footed and bare-chested, and some were down to their skivvies. The earthy-sweet smell of cannabis wafted in from…well… everywhere. The security guards weren't busting anyone; I watched Henry Hart and Gopher Haze share a joint with a uniformed cop. Or someone pretending to be one.

The musicians in The Who were big jazz fans and had invited our band to share their dressing room, which was stocked with all manner of controlled substances. Everything the mind could imagine, the heart could desire, the DA could prosecute, and the coroner could trace in your bloodstream.

Everyone was high. And by the looks of it, planning to stay that way. Maybe forever.

Except for yours truly.

That is, until a voice from the not-too-distant past put my sobriety— and my heart and my libido—on red alert.

Is that you, Blue Carson?

Louise? I said, turning around.

The hottest girl in my eighth grade class stood a few inches in front of me, smiling wildly and looking hotter than ever in her micro-mini skirt and pink go-go boots. With her curly brown hair, her tanned olive skin, her dreamy stoner-red eyes, and her beautiful bare arms folded across her…*beautiful bare breasts.*

I knew I'd find you here! Louise said.

Really? I said. How? Why? When did you… What are you… Louise, I said, where are your clothes?

Oh, I don't know, she said. Out there somewhere. She pointed to the crowd. What difference does it make? Here we are, Blue. Just you and me. She winked seductively. And Chic, she said.

My heart sank. Chic? I said. Chic Chichetti's here, too?

No way! Louise said, laughing. I'm kidding. We broke up ages ago. I haven't seen Chic Chichetti since he stole Mr. Chuli's car on graduation day. And totaled it.

I had the distinct feeling that my life was about to change.

That Chic's as dumb as a bag of doorknobs, Louise said. And a lousy drummer, too. And way too tall. She grimaced. Ever spend two years of your life staring at someone's armpit?

No, I said.

Louise eyed me up and down. Your mother told me you'd be here, Blue. When I called. Last week I called…looking for you.

You did? I said. Why?

I ran into Mr. Burns in Stop & Shop, and he said you were playing with some famous jazz band. I've always admired you, you know. Your music. And your…cuteness. So I flew out to visit my cousin Adrienne, and find you. We sort of crashed through the front door, and here I am. And here you are. Just like Mr. Burns said! Just you and me, Blue. And all these… other people. What a mind fuck, don't you think?

I nodded.

God, I'm so high, Louise said. Don't you want to kiss me, or something?

Yes, I said. I mean, I have to play now, but…yes! Of course, I do. I mean, at some point. Will you wait for me, Louise? Will you be here when I'm done? You could watch the show from backstage. Let me show you where you can—

Oh Blue, you are such a doll, she said. Louise put her arms around my neck and pulled me to her and kissed me on the mouth. It was one of those wet jobs, with lots of tongue and saliva. It was beery sweet and lasted longer than I expected. Way longer. Her skin smelled of pot and flowers. I could feel her breasts pressing into me. It felt just like I'd always imagined it would. Only better.

When we broke to breathe, Louise leaned back and we stared at each other. Then we smiled and sighed in perfect unison. I felt like the only person alive—except for Louise. I stared in amazement at the hottest girl in my eighth grade class, standing there in the flesh. The very same flesh I'd been dreaming about all these years—only it was half naked now instead of fully naked, like in my dreams. I took off my sports coat and draped it over her shoulders. Here, Louise, I said. Put this on and come with me.

I took her by the hand and we walked back to the dressing room and sat down on a couch in the corner. We were alone, but I buttoned the front of the coat anyway to cover her nakedness.

I have to go and play now, I said. Will you be here when I—

Blue, she said, squeezing my hand. Then she closed her eyes. God, I'm so high, she said. Where would I even go?

Our band finished the opening set and the crowd sat there—or laid there—screaming for more. Some tried to stand up and applaud, but couldn't quite make the journey. We played an encore, then another. And as we launched into our third tune, the stage manager ran up to Cootie waving his arms. Thank God, I thought, we're done.

I hadn't been able to concentrate on the music at all. Hadn't heard a note anyone played. I bolted for the dressing room. Louise was lying down on the couch, her head resting on somebody's leg.

I walked over, horn in hand.

Hey, aren't you Keith Moon? I said. The famous rock drummer?

And on't choo Bloo Cahsin? he said. The famous jazz trumboonist?

We shook hands. I nodded to him while eyeing Louise, snoring loudly.

Keith Moon followed my eyes with his. Yor the bloke's gonna take care o' this lit-ul lady when she wakes oop. Right?

I nodded, again. Keith Moon started to laugh and it woke Louise up. She opened her eyes and saw me standing there and reached for me.

Blue! she said. We have to find my cousin. She's gonna be so worried.

Sure, I said. And some clothes.

I'm sorry I fell asleep on you, Mr. Moon, Louise said. It's not that you're boring or anything. I've just never been…this high before.

Keith Moon rose from the couch. No worries, m' deah, he said. Yer a wee bit old f' me, anyways.

We went looking for Adrienne. Minutes later Louise spotted her staggering out of the ladies room, holding Louise's tank top in her hand. Then I proceeded to track down Henry, hoping for some manly advice.

Henry and Adrienne stood eyeing each other, and then Henry—in his infinite wisdom—whistled for a cab, and we all went back to the motel.

It turned out to be an awesomely prodigious night, as you can imagine. During which I evolved in ways I never knew existed. None of them musical.

The next morning, Louise and I stood at the bus, saying goodbye and promising to stay in touch. I told her I'd call and come find her as soon as I got back to Boston, and I meant it. I boarded the bus to cheers and thumbs up and high fives and lots of manly back slapping, as though I'd just won Jazz Player of the Year. It was then I realized that the high from being with Louise would have trumped Jazz Player of the Year hands down.

My life was changing in ways I didn't fully grasp. I sat down and blew on the window and wiped a spot clean, and as the bus pulled away, I looked out at Louise and waved to her till she was out of sight.

When I turned around, Henry was standing in the aisle, extending his arm and holding out the tourniquet.

I sighed. Sorry Henry, I said. I can't be an accomplice to your self-sabotage anymore.

Come on, Little Lord, he said. You owe me. If I didn't set you straight last night you'd still be dreaming about her, instead of—

You're probably right, I said. But the answer's still no.

Henry rolled his eyes and headed down the aisle.

Hey! I called out. I'm just trying to show you some real respect here.

You could never convince me that the primary goal of the Cootie Verman Management Agency wasn't to book consecutive one-night stands at venues located as far apart on the map as possible. Like the one-nighter we did in Detroit, followed by the one-nighter in Dallas (20 hours away), followed by the one-nighter in Miami (22 hours away), followed by the one-nighter in Washington, D.C. (19 hours away), etc. With oppressive mid-summer temperatures, and no hotel stops for days on end, making personal hygiene a losing battle.

Even with every window open to the maximum four inches allowed by design, the odor inside the bus after a few days of stopping only to eat and play the gig and score more drugs, made an acrid attack on your brain through your defenseless nostrils the moment you stepped on board. It was an incessant tangy bouquet of cold dried sweat, hot wet sweat, stale cigarette smoke, fresh cigarette smoke (if there is such a thing), ash- and butt-choked coffee cups, booze breath, empty beer cans and liquor bottles, partially-empty beer cans and liquor bottles, greasy burger remains, cold fries, sticky socks and underwear, hints of mouthwash (mine), hints of aftershave lotion (Henry's), more than hints of flatulence (everyone's)— that had reached critical mass and permeated the molecular structure of everything on the bus. Including the bus.

The days slogged by, as did the nights if we didn't get to de-bus and play a gig. It was during just such a grueling 18-hour haul from Denver to Phoenix that I discovered the surprising depth of perception and intelligence possessed by my drug-addled neighbor across the aisle, Henry Hart.

I've been wondering about something you said, Henry, I said. About thinking while we improvise. Seems like the most natural thing in the world to do. Why's it so bad?

Henry shut off his reading light and closed his little green book. He slid across the seat and leaned into the aisle and put his hand over his mouth so he wouldn't wake the others.

You really want to know? he said.

I nodded.

Here's the first thing you have to know, he whispered. Knowledge can be dangerous. Because the more we know about playing jazz, the more there is to think about while we play it. Sometimes thinking's cool. When it's observational. Or functional. But mostly, it's uncool. Because it leads to emotional judgment, which interferes with…well…everything.

I thought about that for a moment. But what if the emotional judgment is favorable, I said, and the emotion we feel is positive? Joyful even. Wouldn't that energize us in a good way?

Henry shook his head. Judging ourselves emotionally when we play— whether the news is good or bad—is at best a distraction, he said, and at worst an exercise in self-affirmation. Either way, it keeps us out of the zone.

Ah, the mythical zone, I said. I've heard artists and athletes talk about this. How the sense of self magically disappears, and yet the job gets done. Sounds more like an abstraction than a real thing, though.

Oh, the zone is real, Henry said. You can tell by comparing the feeling you have when you're not in it to the one you have when you are. Henry eyed me for a moment. Check this out, he said. When you eat ice cream, do you taste it, or do you think about the taste?

Both, I said.

And where do you think the taste exists?

Inside my mouth, I said.

Inside your brain, Henry said. As neural activity. Which means that you are the taste of the ice cream as much as you are your blood and your bones and your arms and your legs, and any other part of your being.

Uh-huh, I said. So?

So tasting the ice cream and thinking about the taste are two totally different experiences, Henry said. Tasting without thinking about the taste means you're one with the taste. There is no you apart from the taste, and no taste apart from you. There is only—tasting. That is the zone. But thinking about the taste—evaluating it and labeling it—disrupts your oneness with it by creating the impression—some would say the illusion—that there is a taster separate from the taste.

So you're saying that, neurologically speaking, we are the ice cream?

Man-o-man, Henry said, when did you get so smart? But as soon as we say, *This is good ice cream*, or, *This is chocolate ice cream*—there is us on the one hand, and the taste of the ice cream on the other. We're not one with the taste anymore because our thoughts have divided the experience into the taste and the taster.

I sat staring at Henry. What's this got to do with playing jazz? I said.

Think of the sound of a melody or a chord or a rhythm as being like the taste of ice cream. Sound gets transported from a musical instrument through our ears to our brain, where it becomes neural activity that we're one with—like the taste of ice cream—until we label it as Ab or F#, good note or bad note. Now our thinking has divided the experience into the playing and the player, the music and the musician. And instead of being one with the sound, we're separate from it. Locked out of the house, like a cheating husband.

Are you sure about this, Henry? I've never heard it expressed this way before. Sounds very...cosmic.

Henry shot me a wink. Think about how right it feels to lose yourself in the music when you blow that horn. When you disappear into it and become the notes. That's the zone, Blue. I know you know that feeling; there's nothing mythical or unreal about it. Compare that to how it feels to judge yourself and everything you play while you're playing. I know you know that feeling, too.

Guilty as charged, I said.

That's why we seek the zone, Henry said. To be one with the music. And free from the self.

Free from the self, I said. So that's why you called it self-forgetting. Hey Henry, I said, this deserves a book. Or at least a song.

Henry smiled. More? he said.

Why not, I said.

When we're playing in a band, Henry said, and all the players hear the same musical sound but keep from judging it, each player is then one with the same musical sound because their thinking hasn't separated them from it. And through that sound, we become one with each other as well.

Wow, I said. So, experiencing the same neurological information—the same sound, the same music, at the same time—can link us together?

In theory, Henry said, sure. For which the anecdotal evidence is overwhelming.

But Henry, I said, how can you stop your thoughts while you're playing? And how does getting high affect the outcome?

Depending on the circumstances, Henry said, getting high can make it easier for you to ignore or dismiss your thoughts when they start to interfere.

Can? I said. Or does?

The first two times I tried improvising while under the influence I became aware of periods of internal silence in which my thinking seemed to have stopped altogether. This may have happened to me before, but not it a way that I noticed. Maybe it was the drug I took that increased my awareness of it, or maybe it was autosuggestion, I couldn't say. But I also noticed when thoughts did arise in my consciousness while I played, and how some were easy to let go of, while others—especially the emotionally charged ones, whether good or bad—were more tenacious. And distracting.

But the third time I played while high, I had a truly exceptional experience. It felt like a breakthrough of sorts, as far as my improvising was concerned, which I attributed to being in an altered state of consciousness.

At the start of my solo I was serving up my usual jazz vocabulary—a mixture of improvised ideas with an assortment of melodic licks and patterns I had memorized and could employ at will—when suddenly the echo of an idea I had just played kept reverberating in my head, as though it was calling to me. At first I felt nervous, as though the drug I'd taken had made me lose control. But then I relaxed and decided to hang with the idea and see what happened.

I ran with the motive for a few phrases, repeating the rhythm of the idea on the same starting beat of different measures, while adjusting the melody notes by ear to fit the song's changing harmony. Then I played numerous phrases by starting the rhythm of the idea on different beats of the measures, which gave the theme a displaced feeling. When I applied these treatments to fragments of the original idea, I got even more mileage out of it. And by repeating the melodic curve alone of the idea, it was possible to change both the rhythm and the pitches and still hear a connection to the original material. While all this was going on, I periodically recapped the original motive—by playing the original melody notes and rhythmic content on the original starting beat—to remind myself what all the modifications were based on.

Because of how I repeated certain musical elements at different times, the accompanying players could almost predict what was coming next, which enabled them to play in a way that articulated closely with what I played—and sometimes exactly—creating the impression that we were talking to each other through our instruments about the same subject, using the same material.

There was a tremendous buildup of tension and excitement in the music as the solo progressed, since it was all about one single theme, with variations, versus the usual numerous diverse ideas. It seemed to not only attract but hold everyone's attention from the beginning to the end. In other words, because the music was easy to follow, listeners could follow it. And so they did! And when I finally resolved the theme and ended the solo three choruses later, there was a huge impact—a tremendous release of tension, like a tsunami crashing down on the shore—and the audience went wild. The band applauded. Even Cootie stood smiling and shaking his head.

I'm not sure how or why any of this happened, but to me, the solo sounded and felt like nothing I'd ever played or experienced before. It went far beyond demonstrating my ability to play notes and rhythms that fit the meter and chord changes of the song. It felt like a journey, like the unfolding of a multifaceted story, a composition per se, with me as a sort of melodic narrator or navigator—and all of it based on a single inciting event that happened way back at the beginning of the solo.

I thought I had been controlling my playing from one moment to the next by consciously thinking about what to play, but Henry explained it differently.

That wasn't you deciding what to play, Little Lord, he said. Don't get fooled into thinking that your sense of self had anything to do with it. The musical results were too…artistic…to be anyone's intentional doing. It was the absence of you, and the presence of your musicianship alone, uninterrupted by your thinking. If thoughts occurred, they were your ears' thoughts. You were thinking with your ears, man, the way painters think with their eyes.

But isn't that still thinking? I said.

Sometimes thought appears as a mental image, Henry said. Or in the case of music, an aural one. Like a sonogram. We hear an idea as we play it, and then our powers of observation let us reflect on it and hear ahead to what we could play next, giving us the advantage of foresight, and of steering the music. But it's an impersonal act. There's no player separate from the playing, thinking about what to play.

So Henry, I said. Did the drug I took cause this to happen, or help it to?

Henry sighed. Just be on the lookout, he said. Addiction could be the price you end up paying. And trust me, man. The hard stuff is non-negotiable.

In spite of Henry's dire warning, I felt elated. Like I'd just won Jazz Player of the Year while making love to Louise. Maybe I would stay with the band a while longer, I thought, and milk my new discoveries for all the innovation they were worth.

But the very next day, while Henry was up at the front of the bus talking with Gopher about needing a draw on his salary, I noticed his little green book lying on the seat. I stood up in the aisle and reached over and picked it up. There was no printing anywhere on the cover. I opened it to the first page and read the title: *General Theory of Relativity—Albert Einstein.* But the kicker came when I turned to the next page, which was blank except for a handwritten inscription: *To the inspiring jazzman, Henry Hart—a grateful fan, Albert Einstein.*

What are you doing with that, Carson?

I spun around and gulped. Sorry, Henry, I said. I saw it lying there and…I was curious. I'm really sorry.

Henry took the book from my hand. This is none of your Little Lord's beeswax, he said. Did you open it?

I nodded.

See the title?

I nodded.

The inscription?

I nodded.

Do you know what it's about?

All this nodding was making me dizzy. Ultimate reality? I said.

Albert Einstein signed this for my father, Henry said. A better jazz player than I'll ever be.

But how did he—

They met one night when Einstein was living in Princeton. Somehow he wound up in this jazz joint in Trenton where my father was playing guitar.

Oh my god, I said. Did you ever meet him?

Henry shook his head. He played violin, he said. So my dad gave him an album he'd made with Joe Venuti. And Einstein gave him this book.

Do you understand any of this stuff, Henry?

Some of it, he said. It gets clearer with each read. Dad gave it to me before he died, hoping to steer me away from a career in jazz. And drugs. But it hasn't worked. We both failed.

That's ridiculous, Henry, I said. You're a monster jazz player. One of the best I've ever heard. I only hope someday I'll play as good as—

Here, he said, handing me the book. Check it out. Maybe you'll find an alternate career in there somewhere.

Sorry, I said. Math and me…we don't click.

Henry sat down and stared out the window. Save yourself, Blue, he said. Go back to school. Get your degree. Become a teacher. Get married, buy a house, have a family. Gig on weekends.

I cocked my head and looked at him.

Jazz and dope have claimed enough of us, he said.

I didn't know what to say to that. Henry's career advice stopped my thinking cold. Faster and more effectively than any drug could have done it. I realized then that it was going to take time—and the right kind of playing opportunities—to sort it all out.

So, on August 15, 1969, I gave my notice to Gopher Haze.

Vy you vanna do zom zilly zing like zat? Gopher said. Ze fun ist just stahting, Blue. Bezides, Kooti vill vlip hiz lid ven I haz to tellz him!

I knew exactly what to say to that, but I didn't bother.

Two weeks later my tenure with the Cootie Verman organization was officially over. After my last gig with the band, I packed up my horn and said my goodbyes to everyone. It was harder than I thought, especially with Henry and Gopher and Tommy, whose hugs were long and tight.

As I started to leave, Gopher handed me a small paper bag, tied at the top with a piece of colored ribbon. Zo you don' vorget uz, he said.

I opened the bag and reached in and took out the Maxwell House coffee can that had once been full of high-octane Mexican weed.

Aw, gee, you guys, I said. You shouldn't have. I pulled off the plastic lid and looked inside. But…it's empty, I said.

Of course it's empty, Tommy said. What'd ya expect? It's been empty for weeks. We might be dope fiends, but we're not dopes.

Henry winked at me. Anyway, it's the *thought* that counts. Right Doc?

I had to turn away to hide the emotion welling inside.

On my way to the door, I spotted Cootie having a nightcap at the bar. I approached him and said, Well, this is it for me, Cootie. I'm headed back to Boston to finish my degree. Maybe become a teacher. I wish you and the band all the best.

Except for a condescending smirk, Cootie, of course, ignored me. He stood silently sipping his drink, and so I started to walk away.

Oh, I said, I almost forgot. I unzipped my backpack and went back to the bar and set the can of spray paint down next to his drink.

Something to remember me by, I said. I won't be needing it anymore. Then I turned and left.

It took Cootie a second to put two and two together. And as I opened the door to leave, I heard his familiar railing for the last time.

Fuck you, Little Lord! You little punk. I hope you flunk out.

Needless to say, it took all the decency my parents had worked so hard to teach me not to flip Cootie off twice on my way out. Once was all he got.

And around nine months later, I took special pride in denying Cootie his final wish by graduating summa cum laude. I especially enjoyed mailing him a copy of my degree to consummate the victory. And the day after graduation, Louise and I moved from Boston to Providence—where one day I'll get a teaching job and play on weekends and we'll get married and have a family and live happily ever after.

That's what you get for letting your heart and your libido run your life.

Recently, I tried to call Henry to report on my musical progress and invite him up to join me on my weekly gig in town, but his Manhattan number had been disconnected. Then I read in a jazz mag that he was coaching the student jazz ensemble at a community college in Trenton, New Jersey, his hometown. I called the music department and the woman said that Henry no longer taught there. When I asked if she had a number for him, she paused.

Hello? I said. Still there?

So you don't know? she said.

Don't know what? I said.

Did you know Henry very well? she said.

We played together in Cootie Verman's big band, I said. My name's Blue Carson. What do you mean by *did*?

Oh, she said. You're Blue Carson. Henry spoke highly of you.

Spoke? I said.

More silence.

Hello? I said, again.

I'm sorry to be the one to tell you, she said, but Henry passed away.

He what? When? How? Where?

Three weeks ago, she said. Drug overdose. At home, she said.

It was difficult to thank her for the information, and more difficult to hang up the phone. I wanted to ask her questions. About Henry. To ask her what else she knew.

Here we go again, I thought. Another tragic prodigy.

I called Gopher Haze right away and was surprised to catch him at home. Gopher said that Henry had been clean for eight months, and that his curiosity had gotten the better of him one day—as it often does with hardcores—and he took a trip down memory lane. A permanent trip—as it often becomes with hardcores.

Gopher asked me how I was getting along. I tried to put my thoughts about Henry on hold while I told him about setting up house in Providence with Louise. He asked if I'd be interested in hopping back on the band for a world tour.

Just what I need, I said. More hardcore adventures in jazz.

Vee coot use a goot zolovist like you, Blue. Kooti zed I shoot call you. Zed he vill make it verf your vile zis time.

Hell, I said. Without Henry there to watch my back I'd probably end up like all the others. Owing Cootie Verman my next month's salary.

Zink about it, Blue. Ze bus leavz un ten dayz. I vill vatch your back.

I pictured the bus. My seat in the back. Henry's across the aisle. Vacant.

I'll have to run it by Louise, I said.

A long telling silence thundered out from the phone.

Ah, don' vaste your time, Liddle Lawd. Fuck Kooti Verman. Unt fuck jass. Stay home vid Louize and zave yourzelv ze nightmare.

I didn't know what to say to that.

Let me call you, Goph, I said.

We hung up. I sat there in my practice room, holding the phone to my ear and staring at the Maxwell House coffee can perched on top of the piano, still empty. My time on the road flashed before me. I had that feeling again, that my life was about to change. I'd been playing my own solos for a while now. I knew they needed to be heard outside of this room. This flat. This town.

We're all hardcores, I thought, in some respects.

Better to be a tragic somebody than a tragic nobody.

BIG BRAINS IN OUR MIDST

The final leg of our journey began at the peak of the Most Cold Time, as our kind calls it. Winter, as your kind calls it. More final for some, as it turns out, than others. And as I recall it, we started out as four.

But this soon would change.

We joined forces at a kill made high up in the northwest corner of the state, where in the year 2020 the wild is still vast and clean and quiet—if deadly—and on cold clear nights the stars still guide the lone pilgrim along. I never knew where the others came from, or how they got there. I only knew that I once belonged to a family of big brains that had dissolved, and I got sent packing. And that we four shared a similar history, and would likely do better sticking together than going our separate ways in the wild.

The kill was a deer that had been gut shot. A big buck that must have traveled a good and painful distance to elude its tracker before succumbing. Otherwise, it would've been strapped to the carving table of the hopeless big-brain with the miserable aim, and not lying half frozen at our feet. We filled our stomachs quickly, knowing that larger beasts of prey were on the way. And then, as the late afternoon sun melted into the sloping hills of Moosup Valley, we headed for the single beacon of light bleeding through the forest of scrub pine and ash that surrounded us, lighting our way.

We found favor for a time with a young big-brained couple that put food out for us in a three-sided woodshed leaning perilously over the creek. Until one stormy night, when they put it in the back seat of the rusted Volvo parked up by the farmhouse. Once we were inside eating, they snuck up and closed the doors on us and hopped in front and shoved off. Our throaty growls became threatening hisses and then constant warring wails, and after a while the car skidded to a stop. The girl leaned over the seat and opened the door and we all scrambled out onto the shoulder. All but the littlest one, who had to be shooed out. I looked up at the sliver of a moon and felt the heavy wet flakes on my back and opened my mouth and swallowed some to wash down my meager meal. We were in a heavily wooded area at the entrance ramp to a highway. Aw, gee, the girl said. We gotta be goin. Bye-bye, cuties. Then the engine burped and revved and the tailpipe spit out a plume of blackness and she pulled the door shut as they chugged up the ramp and disappeared into that cold dark night.

Earlier that day we had huddled together inside the chicken coop to keep warm, and from there we watched them pack the trunk with their belongings. Frigging water pipes, the boy muttered, kicking the well-house as he passed. Asshole landlords, the girl said. Of course, they would not be taking us with them, nor finding us homes. And the shelter would've been a death sentence. That meant two options: Leave us at an abandoned farm buried deep in the bowels of nowhere, or drop us somewhere closer to civilization—meaning garbage pails—where we might get a crack at other forms of big-brain hospitality.

Same old story. Homelessness is home for the homeless.

These two were always partying and getting high and doing all the crazy things that you big brains do. So I figured we were better off slip-sliding around on iced-covered gravel on our own four feet, than riding in that car with them on four bald tires, in a treacherous winter storm.

Homelessness is fine with me, compared to lifelessness.

Being the oldest and presumably the wisest, I bowed my head to the wind and began leading us down the road, looking for a place to escape under the guard rail where it wasn't packed high and hard with snow. The wind was howling and blowing us every which way, and in the confusion the littlest one lost her bearings and began to cross. I was about to go and get her when I saw lights approaching and heard a vehicle. The horn blared and the brakes screeched and the car swerved and we all dove for cover. Then came a high-pitched squeal—louder than you would have thought—and that was that.

We made it safely to a nearby overpass and took shelter inside an appliance carton, trying not to wake the big-brain lying there with its eyes frozen open. It took a minute, but sleep finally came, and with it the usual welcomed relief. With plump blind mice darting cluelessly through my dreams, evading capture in reality-defying ways.

Next morning we woke with the sun and quickly set out into its warmth. We came upon the entrance ramp where we'd been let loose and stood watching the crows go at her. Her bottom half just a flattened reddish-brown smudge on the dirty-white blacktop. I took a chance and charged, hissing and growling ferociously. But these birdbrains were not going to be scared off. Like us, they were too hungry to be afraid.

Down to three, we were.

For hunting and killing, three is better than two; but for filling your belly, two is better than three. As was often the case, the smallest one wasn't strong enough to fight for his share of the kill—when we were lucky enough to make one. We watched him grow weak, and then one night he didn't come on the hunt. When we returned, he had left the hollow. Later we found him in a ditch by the side of the road. Two deep punctures in his back, the hair and skin scraped from his neck and shoulders, his nose oozing a slimy red goo. Chased into traffic, I figured. By God knows what, I figured. If there is a God, I figured.

My sole companion and I cleaned up his wounds as best we could, while waiting for the life force to decide. Come on, I thought. Make up your damn mind. Empty stomachs heed no rules. When the steam no longer shot from his nose and mouth, we looked at each other and sniffed at the remains. Then we ate him. Had we not, others would have. And instead of us benefitting from a warm and nourishing meal, it would have been them.

Us or them. It's that simple in the wild.

I hate to go spouting cliches, but it really is a jungle out there. A do-or-die, eat-or-be-eaten, survival-of-the-fittest, catch-me-if-you-can, dog-eat-dog jungle. Unlike your kind, however, our kind doesn't take it personally. Or emotionally. We deal matter-of-factly with the endless vicissitudes of life. Without keeping score. Without fretting over the outcome. Without taking credit or casting blame. And, most impressively, without guilt. We feel the thrill of victory and the sting of defeat, of course, but only momentarily. And viscerally. We don't tally up the highs and lows—the gains and losses—and store them in some imagined, anxiety-ridden future. Due to our smaller (and in many ways superior) brains, things just are what they are for our kind. That is our first and only takeaway.

We were but two now. Making our way south through the wooded western borderlands of the untamed Rhode Island wild.

My sole companion was a young, fierce warrior/hunter. Like me, well-advanced for our kind. For any kind. Her self-awareness had been progressing rapidly, with me guiding it along. Indeed, as her mentor in all things cerebral, I had no doubt her sense of connection to all things would someday surpass my own, and possibly match that of the trees. Having never been handled by the big brains in her midst, she was still one with her ancient instincts. Through which she accessed the power of the ages, and—as I instructed her—applied it to her own consciousness. Whereas, despite my supernatural gift (which sometimes feels more like a curse), I had been handled at birth and for a time thereafter, and so had become familiar with the feeling—some would say the indignity—of domestication, as your kind calls it. Lame and tame, as our kind calls it.

She has a smooth, thick, shiny black coat with a collar and slippers of pearly white; whereas mine has become a uniformly dull brownish black, threadbare from age and the wear and tear of staying alive in the wild. And her teeth—those long deadly fangs you glimpse when she yawns or tears into prey—what fearsome weapons they are. Whereas mine—but for a few—are broken off or worn down to nubs from ages of night-long battles and bad diet. Or no diet. Her claws have the strength of bone and are as sharp as the razor wire I taught her to avoid when stalking the fowl pens; whereas mine might take me partway up a tree—or not—before giving out. Yet they can still rob the sight from a snooping rat, or a yearling fox or owl on the attack.

One day, while at the pond, I gazed at our reflections in the water and noticed our eyes were the exact same golden green. Though hers bore a vividness that mine had lost long ago to illness. Diabetes. And FIV (Feline Immunodeficiency Virus, aka Feline AIDS), so I later learned from a big brain your kind calls Dr. Brown. But the size and shape and muted coloring of our eyes was enough to make me wonder if we were related somehow. Siblings, perhaps? Father and daughter, maybe? Then my aches and pains chimed in and declared—*more like great grandfather and…* Whatever.

My only advantage would seem to be my abundant experience of living in the wild, which she is keen enough to know would count for far more than just…well, for more than just experience. Oh yes, and my not-so-secret weapons—my prodigious jowls, which make me look larger and meaner and fiercer than I could ever pretend to be. And my savage warring cry—a bloodcurdling, spine-tingling, guttural wail, conjuring the image of a fearsome beast of prey. Perfected while I was still a young stud on the prowl, and which is sometimes menacing enough to end a conquest before it begins. It even scares me on occasion, when I really let loose.

By comparison, her wincing wail has never matured, and remains a thin, stunted, strained, scratchy whine. The advantage of which is that it suckers rivals into thinking she is weak. Or afraid. Little do they know the extent of the bloody life lesson that awaits them in a serious tangle.

Eventually we reached the coast, where we settled in and braved the elements out on a densely forested and sparsely populated peninsular your kind calls Indian Bluffs. And there we waited for the Warm Time, as our kind calls it. Spring, as your kind calls it. And as I recall it, our good fortune prevailed.

But good fortune only means one thing: Bad times lie ahead. And since our kind doesn't value Time the way yours does, a typical small brain's knowledge of how long our luck lasted would be but a rough estimate.

Your kind thinks more highly, and hence more accurately, of Time and other such relative or abstract measurements. A dubious advantage of your big brains. Being the astute observer that I am, I might use my grasp of your big-brained skills to tell you precisely how long we prospered, but there is the ever-present danger of becoming more like you from thinking and acting as you do. And as my understanding of your big-brain ways deepens, so does my concern (as a quasi-big-brain, myself) that they may one day involuntarily trump my preferred small-brain nature.

Your brains may be big, but so is the emotional attachment you suffer because of them. Obsessive emotional attachment—to yourselves, mainly. And to family and friends. Even to what you call your *enemies*—the concept of which (by the way) is entirely foreign to every other life form. We all have predators and competitors in the wild, but they are not our enemies. We may fear them, but we do not hate them. The enmity your kind experiences toward one another is clearly misguided. Big-brained or small, we must all become predators and competitors at times—or perish. Everything must consume *something* to survive, and in turn will be consumed by something *else*. In the process, all is forgiven in the wild. If not forgotten.

Besides, does size really matter? Brain-size, I mean. Is bigger really better?

Let's see.

Your big-brained emotional attachment extends even to your reputations. Your successes and your failures. Your possessions and your wealth. And to the past. Your should haves and could haves. Even to the future. Your hopes and dreams. All of which generates enough tension and stress to support an entire industry's worth of therapies and addictive medications. Your kind laments the past and fears the future because you have no idea how to live in the present, where the only real living takes place. The infinite and eternal now is but a myth to your kind. A brief moment the future tramples on and hurries through to become the past.

Our small-brain actions rule our lives and determine how we think; your big-brain thoughts rule your actions and determine how you live. You crave security, for example, of which there is none; and fail to embrace uncertainty, though all life is rooted in it. And you are supposed to be the smart ones! Which, admittedly, in some ways you are. But stupidly so. You create affordable housing, for instance. Central air. Art. Medicine. Food banks. Medicare. Social Security. Little Friskies. The Humane Society. And so on. But you don't stop there. You create politics—and worse, politicians. Religion—complete with saints and sinners, and the kids: Good and Evil.

You create war. Pollution. Climate change. Big Pharma. Artificial Intelligence—to replace the real stuff, I suppose, which hasn't exactly been a boon to existence either. Social Media, and that Zuckerberg character. God—or worse, Frump, who fancies himself one. The Devil—or worse, McCon-Well, completing the course in record time and graduating top of his class.

The list goes on. Hypocrisy. Duplicity. Guile. Theme parks. Lite beer. Smooth jazz.

And slavery? Really? Zoos alone should have disqualified you.

You split the atom and use the energy to power cities, but also to build bombs with which you destroy them. Then you dump the nuclear waste into the ocean, or bury it in the earth, where it poisons the planet we all inhabit and threatens your very own existence.

You live in desperate isolation, terrified of your own shadows. United only by that which you most wish to be separate from.

You strive to control the so-called civilized world and then bilk it of its natural resources, ignoring the necessity for sustaining the mutually dependent ecosystems of the wild. Your greedy corrupt nature will not let you live in peace. Endless unrest is the price you must pay—the price we *all* must pay—for your big brains.

In fact, this big brain of yours—with its myriad unnatural appetites—is the only truly regrettable natural development produced by the evolution of life thus far.

But a few of you have a bit of us in you still. Some of our natural grace was passed on to your kind when you descended from us eons ago, and a tiny percentage of you have grasped the unequivocal rightness of it.

Against all odds, my companion and I have recently come across just such a creature. Our name for her is Pure Being, but your kind calls her Joys—an appropriate name, in that she appears to feel joy from everything she encounters. Even from vegetation—and especially the trees, wisest of all life forms, having discovered how to communicate through underground root systems. She even feels joy from us, who she now considers family. Then she transmits the joy back to its source, without even realizing she's doing it, or so we suspect. Indeed, she seems closer to our kind than to yours.

She has names for us, too. I am Johnna, or Simba, or Green-Eyed Monster. But, mostly, I am John. My companion is Shu-Shu, or My Girl, or *No! Not Another Bunny!* But, mostly, she is Sharon.

John and Sharon. These are the names we go by now.

And as we sit here sunning on the back deck of the cozy country cottage we now call home, gazing out at Joys's lush and colorful garden—with its red brick walkways and flower-covered trellises and wooden arbors, and its wrought iron obelisks and stone sundials and bubbling water fountains, and its sculpted birdbaths and humming wind chimes and squirrel-proof bird feeders—while enjoying the comfy, tattered, wicker couches and chairs in which Sharon has been lounging and casually eyeing a male cardinal—I would now like to invite my companion to say a few words.

Is there anything you would like to add at this juncture, Sharon? In your own untamed, unbridled, and unorthodox fashion?

Yes! Sharon want say, John say too many long time. Too many blah blah blah! No smart say mean thing big brain. No persuade. Only polarize. Make big pain in big brain.

Whoa! Polarize. Persuade. Where'd you pick up those beauties?

Sharon many fan Justice Truth-Bearer Gives-Birth.

But Ruth Bader Ginsberg was an exception, Sharon. Like Joys. Your typical big brain needs hourly reminders of the chaos and havoc—

Truth-Bearer many exception, yes. Truth say Frump no God. McCon-Well no Devil. Only pawn Big Business. Many blind ambition.

Sharon, do you know why God created snakes before he created politicians?

Snake many creepy.

Because he needed the practice!

Why John say he? Maybe God she. Maybe is God, maybe is no God.

Never mind, Sharon. It's a joke, for heaven's sake. You don't know what you're missing if you can't enjoy a little cutting-edge sarcasm now and then. You need to work on that.

John need work on no say mean far right, say confuse far right. Poor far right. Far right many fear. Nature nurture many mean them.

Okay, I knew I shouldn't've brought up politics. How about we just keep it simple and straight to the point. Let's just stick to the story, Sharon.

John say many no simple! Many no point. Many no story. Now my say.

But Sharon, these big brains aren't used to this broken English. This Sharon speak. It's very hard to understand.

Sharon English no broke! John ear broke.

I'm sorry, Shu-Shu, but—

Fine. Sharon say only story. We sees Joys in Warm Time. In big garden. Joys tall friend name Hel. Hel face touch Joys face. Joys say haha, Hel say haha.

Pardon me for interrupting, but what Sharon is saying is that we came across Joys in the spring—Joys and her mate, a tall male your kind calls Hel. They were strolling together in the garden—which, by the way, has every type of botanical treasure you can imagine. There's oak-leaf hydrangeas, autumn-blooming clematis, Rose of Sharon, Korean spice viburnum. She's got peonies, spirea, lambs ear, azaleas. Russian sage, crape myrtle, wild geraniums. Smoke bushes, iris, day lilies. And everyone's favorite—thalictrum! It's a true testament to Joys's love of nature, and nature's love of Joys. Anyway, they were strolling along, laughing and kiss—

John show off! Sharon many claw.

Okay, sorry. Go ahead, then, Sharon. We're listening.

Butterfly go Joys. Joys talk butterfly. Every eyes surprise! Bird come. Joys talk bird. Bird no fear Joys. Then beast come. Joys talk beast. Beast no fear Joys. Joys talk bird. Talk beast. Talk bug, talk plant, talk tree. Talk all! Joys no big-brain kind. No small-brain kind. Joys own special brain kind.

Excuse me, Sharon. Let me explain this in words the big brains will—

After Warm Time go, Hot Time come. Food many easy. We leave Joys and Hel house. Roam many place.

Sharon…please. I think you should let me—

Cool Time come, we go far place. Still many eat every food time.

She's talking about Fall now, when the weather is perfect for roaming the wild. We left Joys and Hel's place, which is tucked away deep in the woods, with ocean on three sides. It overlooks this little cove where—

Cold Time come! We not eat many. Most Cold Time come. We no eat every food time. Belly many pain. We roam back Joys and Hel.

I'll take over now, Sharon. These poor big brains will never be able to—

HISSSSSSS! Sharon many fang.

Okay, okay. I see them.

Joys feed bird every food time. We hide bush. Sharon catch bird every food time. John sleep, mouth catch fly. Sharon kill beast every food time. John sleep, kill time. Sharon give many food John every food time.

Well, yes, it's true that Sharon does have the speed and the power and the cunning—

Every food time Joys bring food. Talk many sweet us. We eat many. Joys try touch. One time John not so fear. Joys touch John!

Well, you know, by then I could tell that Joys could be trusted. And since I'd been handled by big brains before—

John no fear. I still fear. I want Joys touch. One time Joys bring food, I not so fear. I feel trust. Joys try touch. I try trust.

See? Sharon needed me to show her how to trust, how to deal with—

Then Joys touch. I trust. I no fear Joys! Only fear Hel.

Hah! Now she fears Hel. Can you believe this?

Yes, John. Big brains many believe this. Hel talk us. New talk than Joys. Soft air talk.

Please! Sharon. Pretty please with baby bunnies on top. The word big brains use for 'soft air talk' is whisper. Hel talked in calm quiet whispers so we'd relax and trust him. Big brains call that a cat whisperer.

Hel bring food every food time. Talk soft air whisper us. We no more fear. We go to Hel.

Hah! We go to Hel! She doesn't get your big-brained concept of hell. No surprise there. Only your kind could dream up a celestial torture chamber to punish yourselves eternally with…

Hey…Sharon…what's wrong? Why are you looking at me like that?

John say many mean thing. End sentence many preposition.

I'm just trying to help these big brains see the folly of their ways. And okay, let's talk prepositions. In your case, the utter lack of them.

Sharon only say need. John always need say.

Are you calling me a big-mouthed wise guy?

Wise, no. Mouth big, yes.

Now look here, Sharon…

Sharon done story. Go find bird.

Slow down, Shu-Shu. Give me a chance—

John many slow poke. Bird many haha.

You'll never nab that cardinal, Sharon. He's too smart and too fast.

Sharon hide bush. Wait bird.

Hey, look who's up on the deck.

John shhh. Talk soft air me. Waiting bird.

It's Joys and Hel. Listen. They're talking about us.

Have you seen the cats, Hal?

Yes, Joyce, they were here a little while ago. John asleep in the food bowl. As usual. Sharon studying the cardinal. God, that bird's days are so numbered.

How long ago was it, exactly?

Oh, I don't know. Back when the coffee pot whistled. Five minutes ago. Why? What's the matter now?

Mr. Donelli called and said he saw the foxes in his yard.

Just now, you mean? This morning?

Said he counted five of them. The dad, the mom, and three big pups.

Damn. They could be headed here. We better start looking.

He said something got to his chickens last night. He thinks it was the fisher cat.

The one he caught on video? With the pigs? Did he catch it on video last night, too?

No, he said the camera wasn't working.

How does he know it was the fisher then, and not the foxes?

Some of the chickens were unhurt. Some were half dead. And the fully dead ones hadn't been eaten or carried off. Just killed. And left there.

I'm telling you, Joyce, we need to call Animal Control. Get them to trap that thing and get rid of it somewhere. What if it's rabid? What if it attacks some kid? What if it attacks you in the garden? What if it attacks—

You—on the couch? They can't just catch it and drop it off someplace, Hal.

Well, the cats might be able to keep a fox at bay, but forget a fisher. They're vicious killers, Joyce. And that one old man Donelli caught on film is a huge male. You saw the video. It didn't kill those pigs out of hunger. More like sport. Looked like it was enjoying itself.

I know. It terrifies me. I don't even want to go for our walks at night anymore.

Maybe I can ask Howard Cole if he'll lend me one of his AK47's for protection.

Stop it, Hal. It got the Coles' poodle, you know.

Yeah, I know. When did you find out?

Lorraine told me last night. I would've said something when I got home, but you were asleep. When did you find out?

I saw Howard at CVS. He didn't offer any details, but he seemed upset. We haven't been talking much since he came out as a Trump supporter.

Poor Lorraine was a mess. She said Howard let Skippy out around six Wednesday night, and a few minutes later they heard barking and growling. Then these awful howling and yelping noises. They found Skippy at the end of the driveway in a puddle of blood. His entrails torn out.

Jesus, Joyce, that's a fisher. Remember the rabbit skins we found in the garden? Nothing left inside them, not even a skeleton. And Skippy would've fought back. He's a good-size dog. Was.

Okay. Now I'm scared. We have to find the cats.

Has John had his insulin?

No. He needs his shot by eight or it'll screw up the schedule again. And I don't want another diabetic episode like the last one.

What time is it now, Joyce?

Seven fifty-five. That coma was a nightmare. The poor thing almost—

You mean the expense was a nightmare.

I don't care how much it costs, Hal. These cats have come too far. If we can help them live halfway decent lives...

Let's be real, Joyce. John's diabetes is incurable. To the tune of two costly insulin shots per day, which only you can give him. We can't leave town for more than a few hours at a time, so forget traveling during retirement. We're hostage to a decrepit feral cat. Not to mention the AIDS will get him if the diabetes doesn't. And now Sharon's got a urine infection, according to the bloody pee stains on the couch. For which we didn't buy fabric protection because of the extra cost. Face it, these animals are a mess. Like our furniture. And our social lives.

Those were accidents, Hal. She tried to wake us up.

She's a wild animal. She won't use a litter box. And what's gonna happen when it gets cold and we don't have the heart to put her out? More pee stains? Plus she's probably full of worms. And fleas. And we're the only ones who can get near her. Even the vet's afraid to handle her.

That vet caused more problems than Sharon did, Hal. He's not an animal person. He's not a person person either. We'll take them to Dr. Brown, the one who neutered them. She's brilliant. And kind. And—

Expensive.

We can afford it.

We could've afforded fabric protection, too.

Please. Not now. Just help me find them.

Johnnnn-yyy! Come on, Simba. Sharrrrr-onnn! Come get your foodie, Shu-Shu.

Shake the bowl, Joyce. So they hear the food banging around.

Can you call Mr. Donelli, Hal? See if he's seen them?

Don't worry, he'll call us if he sees them. Or rather, you. That old coot's got a thing for you, Joyce, in case you haven't noticed. Always talking about your hair. *Oh the silvery whiteness of it.* And your clothes. *How great you look in everything. Anything. Nothing.* God knows what he's got on his mind.

Who are you calling an old coot, Hal? Tom Donelli is only 73 years old. You're 70, for heaven's sake. Or have you forgotten already?

How do you know how old he is? And why's he telling you his age? He looks a helluva lot older than 73, is what I think

He's a handsome man for any age, is what I think.

Oh really? Is that what you think?

Not as handsome as you, but—

Don't be fooled by that gigolo, Joyce. Three years makes a deal-breaking difference at this stage of the game.

Let's just find the cats, okay?

Maybe we should call the Trump supporters and let them know our cats are missing. I mean, in case Howard mined the driveway with C4. Or put out fisher bait laced with ricin.

Lorraine is not a Trump supporter, Hal. And Howard's on the fence now. The virus has him reconsidering.

Reconsidering what? Which germs to shoot? Let me tell you something, Joyce. Any full-grown adult person who brags about keeping two loaded AK47s under the bed, and wears Army fatigues every day but was never in the military, is just too scary not to be a Trump supporter.

Look Hal, there's John. Under the arborvitaes. Sharon's with him. Oh no, she's got something.

Shit, it's moving.

Is it alive? Oh, please say yes.

Well, if it's moving you can assume—

Sharon! No!

She dropped it, Joyce. It's trying to get away. She's playing with it.

Come here, Shu-Shu. Have some foodie.

She grabbed it again. It's a rabbit. A baby.

No! Not another bunny! She must've found a nest.

Shake the food bowl louder, Joyce, so she'll—

I'm shaking it, Hal. Can't you hear that? Where's John?

Sitting behind her. Watching the slaughter. Not lifting a finger, as usual.
The rabbit's lucky day.

I need to corner him so he'll come to me… Johnnna! Good boy, Simba.

He's coming out by the shed, Joyce.

Come, Johnna. Want some foodie? Oooff! Gotcha.

Watch his claws, Joyce. Don't let him scratch you.

He's not gonna scratch me. What a good boy my Johnny is. Come on,
let's go do your shot and be done with all this drama.

Until tonight, you mean.

That's right. Until tonight. And don't listen to that jealous old meanie,
Johnna. Why should he worry, I'm the one who takes care of you, right?
Him, too.

Just shoot him up quick, Joyce. Before he goes comatose and we have
to remortgage the house.

There's Sharon, Hal. At the birdbath. What's she got now?

Shit.

What is it?

The cardinal.

No! Not the cardinal! Stop her.

So, Sharon, how was food time today?

Beast no many meat. Cardinal many bone. Belly many empty.

How come you didn't share with me? Was it something I said?

John say many no smart. Many interrupt.

Well, I'm sorry you feel that way. How did you feel when Hel told Joys
what a nuisance we are?

Fine. Joys optimist. Always half glass full. Hel pessimist. Always half glass empty.

Well, I personally think we should be prepared for the worst. You can't trust these big brains completely. One minute they love you, the next minute—

John many cynic. Always who peed glass?

I'm just being cautious. And you're being gullible.

Sharon Buddhist. *Is* no glass.

Hey, there goes Joys and Hel on their walk. Let's follow them.

Night many dark. Woods many creature. No many safe.

Yeah, but...suppose they need our help.

John go. Sharon stay.

Come on, Shu-Shu. Where's your sense of adventure? Sharon many Buddhist. *Is* no glass. *Is* no dark. *Is* no creature...

Do you really think it's okay to walk this path at night, Hal?

It'll be fine, Joyce. I've got a flashlight. You made junior varsity wrestling. Maybe the fisher got into Howard's ricin treats. Or tripped a mine in the driveway. Or drowned in the moat.

Lorraine and Howard are not bad people, Hal. You said yourself you're not voting for Biden, just against Trump. At least they listen to what other people have to say.

Yeah, and then burn a cross on the lawn if they don't like what they've heard. Paint a swastika on the door.

That's not funny, Hal. The Coles aren't like that. I'm not listening to you anymore. I'm turning off my cochlear implant... Mmm, the silence is wonderful. What an improvement.

We'll go as far as grandpa Donelli's place, Joyce. You can wave goodnight from the road to your not-so-secret ancient admirer.

Sorry, I can't hear you.

Or maybe we'll tempt fate and walk down to the Coles' bunker, and hope we don't get blown to Kingdom Come. Those revolving search lights Howard installed to spot enemy aircraft should keep away any deadly varmints.

I wouldn't count on that, Hal. Tom said the floodlights were blazing in the yard when the fisher attacked.

Tom? Now it's *Tom*? I thought his name was old man Donelli.

Stop it. Please.

Hey, what was that noise?

I didn't hear anything.

Turn on your cochlear, Joyce.

It's on. It's been on. How else could I have heard what you… Are you trying to scare me?

I think we better head home. You can call gramps when we get there and say goodnight.

I'm good with that. Wouldn't want to keep a handsome man like Tom Donelli from his beauty sleep.

You both better keep moving. And step on it.

Who said that? I know that voice.

It's Howard. I'm not trying to frighten you two, but you shouldn't be out here right now.

Howard, what on earth are you doing hiding in the bushes?

I'm not hiding, Joyce. I'm waiting. For the right moment.

What…right…moment?

Let's go, Joyce. I'm not interested in finding out what right moment Howard's waiting for. In the middle of the woods.

I was emptying the garbage and I heard something prowling around in the yard. I followed it out here. To this tree.

My god, Howard. Why would you do that? Where's Lorraine?

I need closure, Joyce. Wouldn't you? If it got your cats?

If what got our cats?

The fisher that killed Skippy is up in this tree. Just above our heads.

The what? Is where?

So you two best keep moving. Before it drops down here and—

Howard, that thing is evil incarnate. It's not afraid of you.

Don't worry, Hal. That's why I've got this.

You've got an assault rifle? You brought an AK47? What are you going to do with that thing, Howard, shoot the woods down? Create a war zone? Right here on Ridge Rock Road?

Howard, please. We can call Animal Control in the morning.

No, Joyce. That's not the way this going to end.

But they have the methods and the means to—

Jesus, let's go, Joyce. Good bye, Howard. Happy assaulting.

Judging by the mood that filled the house when we got back from the walk, it looked like Sharon and I were grounded for the night.

Joys no talk. Hel talk only Hel. Sharon squat couch, Hel many No, no, no! We speed door. Joys many Come back! John medicine time!

The next thing we knew, the floodlights had lit up the yard like a car lot. And from our hiding place under the arborvitaes, we could hear Joys and Hel shaking the food bowls and calling for us. After a while, we got curious about the portly big-brain in the jungle getup—the one your kind aptly calls How-Odd—so we took off to find him. Sure enough, he was standing where we left him, shining a light up into the branches of a tall cherry tree.

We hide bush. Watch How-Odd. We sees moving thing in tree. How-Odd hold big stick. Point stick moving thing. Stick make pop-pop noise. We many fear.

Well, of course we were afraid. We'd never heard gunfire like that before.

How-Odd look tree. Tree many moving. Moving thing jump down.

How-Odd was right, it was the fisher cat. I'd never seen such a big one. Part weasel. Part wolverine. All warrior. With its snout raised and wrinkled up, flashing its saber-like fangs. I thought it would make a run for it. But instead, the brazen beast started circling How-Odd.

How-Odd say many mean thing moving thing. Moving thing many snarl How-Odd.

How-Odd brought the gun to his shoulder. But before he could shoot, the fisher leaped and landed on his leg.

How-Odd fall down. Moving thing many growl, many bite. How-Odd many scream. Many freak out.

I had had enough at this point, and was about to haul my small-brained butt out of there, when Sharon dove onto the fisher's back and started clawing its face, going for the eyes. I knew she was no match for this thing alone, so I lunged for its tail and bit into its hindquarters and began strafing its scrotum with my rear claws. The fisher roared and brayed as the blood flowed.

Sharon find eyes. Moving thing many pain. Then moving thing find Sharon.

That's when Joys and Hel got there. Joys rushed to help How-Odd. Hel grabbed How-Odd's gun. The fisher had pinned Sharon to the ground. I was clinging to its tail, clawing furiously at its underbelly.

Shoot the fisher, Joys screamed.

I might hit Sharon, Hel screamed back.

Moving thing go many wild. Sharon many pain. Belly many blood.

Suddenly the fisher had my tail between its jaws. I reached for its snout and raked it with my claws. Then I saw Hel—pointing the gun at the treetops.

Fire stick make many pop-pop noise. Every beast many fear. Moving thing run woods.

Hel fired at the fisher as it bumped into trees and bushes trying to escape. When it had disappeared into the brush, Hel laid the gun down and gave Joys his belt. Joys tied How-Odd's leg in a tourniquet to stop the bleeding. Hel took Sharon in his arms.

Easy, Shu-Shu, Hel said. Damn thing got you good.

Joys came and got me. Oh my god, Johnna, she said. Your tail. Where is it?

The fisher had bitten it clean off. Joys saw it lying curled up in the dirt and picked it up and stuffed it into her pocket. I thought I saw it twitching.

We gotta get you out of here, Simba, she said. You guys need a doctor.

Hel stood looking at How-Odd and shaking his head. I'll get the truck, he said. You can't walk on that leg. He handed How-Odd the AK. Take this, Hel said, in case it comes back for you. If I was that thing, I know I would.

Wait, How-Odd said. What if it returns?

Consider it closure, Hel said. That's what you wanted, right?

Sharon had regained consciousness by the time we got back to the house. Hel laid her in a box and set it next to him on the front seat of the pickup. Joys sat beside it, holding me in her lap while she dialed the hospital. I looked into the box and meowed. Sharon gazed up at me and opened her mouth. I half expected to hear her thin, stunted, scratchy whine. Or at least some soft air whisper talk. But not this time. I sat there licking the blood from my tail bone, listening to her labored breathing. And then we took off.

We dropped off trigger-happy How-Odd at the ER, and then we met Dr. Brown at her office. She took one look at Sharon and whisked her away. Later she came back and sewed my tail on. Then she fitted me with a clear plastic collar—aka the cone of shame—so I wouldn't rip out the sutures with the teeth I no longer had, having left them in the fisher's rump. Not wanting to cause a scene, I waited till we got home and then I tugged and clawed at the blasted thing around my neck till I broke free. Joys and Hel were too busy worrying about Sharon to notice, or to care. She would be spending the night—and then some—with Dr. Brown.

Hey guys, I thought. Didn't I just save the day, too?

According to my big-brain calculations, it's been three weeks now since How-Odd's lunatic assault on the fisher. I'm sure Sharon would've wanted me to tell you that she hung on as long as she could. As courageous and noble in death as she was in life. *No! Not another bunny!* is probably eyeing some poor cardinal right now, in that great big Wild in the sky.

I'm happy to say my tail is finally working again—relieving the body's nervous energy by involuntarily snapping and swiping at nothing in particular. Just today, while sunning on the deck, it caught my attention and I began chasing it around. I was surprised to find it was more work than it used to be, the way it winded me. Must be catching up to old man Donelli, if I haven't already passed him.

Lying there panting away, I spotted something moving in the garden. I watched the sporadic movements of the leaves and bushes for a while, but nothing appeared. Curious, I snuck down the stairs and into the backyard, and as I stepped onto the brick walkway I spied the fisher, digging for grubs under a hosta plant. He lifted his disfigured snout into the air and sniffed. My first instinct was to bolt, but then I saw the two scarred holes where his eyes should have been. He wasn't completely blind, it seemed, but enough to not see me standing frozen on the spot.

I smiled to myself, thinking of how his days of procreating were done for after the nasty clawing I'd given his manhood. As were his days of stalking and preying on innocents, after the job Sharon did on those eyes. It is what it is in the wild, I thought. I had no doubt, however, that he could still decimate anything he had the opportunity to sink those claws and teeth into. He was, after all, a fisher cat.

As I cautiously watched him, a strange thing happened. My ears began to get hot. The feeling then spread to my neck, and down into my shoulders and chest, and then the skin all over my body began tingling and radiating heat. My fur was standing on end and my mouth had gone dry. I was out of breath, panting again. This—I surmised—was anger. Not the momentary pang of it my small brain was used to, but the relentless, mindless, self-poisoning, big-brained version your kind is so well-known for. And good at.

Things had become personal. There was a score to settle here. This beast had killed my companion, and though it was a fair fight—five of us plus the AK47 against one—I wanted payback. To hell with my small-brain superiority, I thought. To hell with all is forgiven in the wild. I will whip up a heaping plate of hot-and-heavy big-brain-style revenge on this son-of-a-bitch. Or die trying.

And don't worry, I haven't forgotten about the real culprit in this saga, Mister Menace himself: How-Odd the Nut Job.

I had always worried that, due to my supernatural gift/curse, I might one day become so infected with your big-brain ways that I wouldn't be able to choose anymore; that your ways would overcome my small-brain nature and eliminate the option. Well, I'm not worried about it anymore, because that day has arrived.

Now the plan is to let the fisher catch my scent, and then lead it via fake cries of distress through the woods and into How-Odd's backyard, where every afternoon he sits napping in a wheelchair, facing west to glimpse the setting sun. Hence, my approach will be from the east, with the fisher stalking just a few feet behind. And as How-Odd lays down the AK to welcome me onto his lap—as he typically does in gratitude for helping to save his sorry life—retribution will be close at hand.

All I have to do is work out my escape plan. Or, maybe not. As Hel likes to say: If the diabetes doesn't get him, the AIDS will. Call me small-brained, but who wants to lie around helplessly while some hideous disease picks you apart? Where's the glory in that? The dignity? If I can choose, let it be the fisher. Or How-Odd's AK, even. Let it be the Wild itself that puts an end to my big-brain days.

And can't you hear Sharon right now?

John say many blah blah blah.
No persuade. Only polarize.
Make big pain in big-brain.

As I said in the beginning, this was the final leg of our journey. More final for some, as it turns out, than others. And as I recall it, we started out as four.

Down to one, we are now.

But this soon may change.

COVID SERENADE

S aving the world is not easy. And it's not always fun, either. Success depends so much on *you*—as in, do you want to be saved? All I can do is blow my horn and play my music (the fun part), and hope you'll hear it and become inoculated like the others (the tough part). Otherwise, you'll risk becoming a Spreader. And, not to be an alarmist, but I've heard rumors that—with so much at stake now—the powers-that-be may decide to eliminate the Doubters and Deniers out there, if they don't hurry up and get on board.

I wish we'd figured it out sooner, because all it takes is two one-hour-long sets. About twelve tunes, tops, with solos. It's fast and free and relatively painless. With minimal side effects. Unless you start feeling a sudden urge to play jazz, in which case you should call 911 and seek medical attention immediately.

Think of the first set as the first dose, and then later on you check out the second set—the second dose, the booster shot, if you will—and it's done. You're vaccinated. Immune. Free to do what you want with your life, as long as it doesn't harm anyone or anything else. Like in the old days, back when humanity still had a fighting chance. Before Nature decided the world had suffered enough because of us, and, in self-defense, sent in the Virus to cull the crop. Clean up the mess we'd made of everything—the climate, the land, the air, the food, the water, the wildlife, the peace. And then added those pesky Variants to make sure we don't make a comeback and ruin things all over again. I've heard the latest mutation causes brain tumors that can make the victim hallucinate till their head explodes.

You can't blame Nature for this; She's no dummy. There just aren't enough good reasons to trust human beings to do the right thing anymore. The way we've behaved so far, you'd think that humanity itself was a virus. And yet, my friends and I are hopeful that—with cooperation—we'll be able to turn things around and avoid that horrible legacy. Because I, Sister Angelique Victoria Etwombe (SAVE)—a middle-aged jazzbo living in a two-room flat on a meager unemployment check, with the jazz chops to match—will soon be representing humanity at the upcoming conference on Ultimate Strategies (US), during which the fate of humankind will be decided.

Now, I know what you're thinking: She's a jazz player. Must be high on drugs. Probably bad ones. Cheap ones, anyway, for sure.

But no, I don't do drugs. Never have. As cheap as the bad ones might be, I could never afford them. Still can't.

The hole-in-the-wall barroom where I play once a week—and where my friends Yin and Yang first appeared to me in their humanoid forms—is called The Lowered Bar. And if you saw the place, you'd know why: The proverbial bar doesn't go any lower. It's on Wickenden Street in Providence, Rhode Island (State Appetizer: fried calamari), located in a quaint old neighborhood on the east side of town. Complete with junk shops and bars and book stores and historic houses. And tall trees and foreign food joints and crazy college kids and churches with names you don't recognize.

My gig streams live from the bandstand via Zoom every Tuesday night, from nine till midnight. I play the saxophone—tenor—alone and in front of a computer that films me playing as it simultaneously plays pre-recorded backing tracks through an external speaker system and sends out the video and audio feeds to whoever might be tuning in. Think of it as jazz's answer to karaoke. With me being the only frustrated wannabe.

I make the musical backing tracks also, by videotaping myself playing all the other instruments in the band. I start with the drum track for each song, which I film myself playing from beginning to end on my drum set at home. Complete with the drumistically correct torn jeans and dirty T-shirt and bare feet and bloodshot eyes and exaggerated facial expressions, showing how cool and into my own playing I am. Then I'll put on shades and a fedora and a zoot suit (so it isn't so obvious it's me) and film myself laying down the bass parts to the drum tracks, showing how hip and stylish and aloof I can be. Then, donning a sexy cocktail dress, I'll add the piano parts to the bass and drum tracks, while gazing up at the ceiling and lolling my head in a jazz-like manner, showing how lost in my own world I can be. And record all that, too.

Then I combine these three videos on a single computer screen with separate viewing windows, and project it onto a life-size screen at the club. Resulting in the kind of full rhythm section accompaniment you'd expect to see and hear in a live jazz performance.

And when I hop on stage and add my sax to the mix during my weekly gig at The Lowered Bar (the video of which is shown in a fourth window, with me wearing a sensibly demure ensemble, showing off how sophisticated and professional and ladylike I can be), and Zoom out the finished product to the world at large, it's like the four of me are performing live in your living room. Demonstrating the kind of musical interaction that we jazz players are known for, as we astonish you listeners with breathtaking displays of instrumental acrobatics and improvisational derring-do.

More or less.

I call the band the Sister Angelique Victoria Etwombe Jazz Quartet— or simply, SAVE JAZZ. When people hear the name, they'll sometimes ask if I am—or ever was—a nun. But the Sister moniker has no religious significance in my case. Far from it. I never mixed well with organized religion. When things like religion get organized by mere mortals (and who else would feel self-important enough to try?), sooner or later politics takes over. And you find yourself having to watch your back all the time, and other parts of your body, too. Or leave the fold, like I did.

Because any organization that protects predatory authority figures lurking within its own ranks has some serious soul searching of its own to do. To paraphrase an American proverb: If God isn't the problem, and people are the problem (like most believers claim), then why call the problem clergy and give them the authoritative power of God?

I know people who say their religion has helped them become a better human being. And if that's true, then I'm glad for them. And for the rest of us, too! But I can't help notice that organized religion doesn't provide a single positive human value that I can't find in my own heart without it.

So, no, the Sister sobriquet is just a handle that fans have used in reference to my gender: Female (the proud, strong, self-sufficient femme fatale variety), and the color of my skin: Ebony (a rich, smooth and creamy dark chocolate, that just makes you want to take a big bite).

Physically, I've got this exotic African vibe happening. I'd have to say that I'm good looking, too. And shapely. But not so much in either category to distract you from my jazz playing. Which I'm thankful for. I'd gladly be ugly as sin if it meant I could play better. Still have my health to varying degrees. Although I have to wonder how that ever happened.

One cheeky thing about this online gig is having to introduce myself to the crowd—virtual though it is nowadays—as the player of each instrument. *How bout a nice hand for Sister Angelique, wailing away on drums*, I'll say. *Folks, that was Sister Angelique*, I'll say, *tearing it up on bass. Ladies and gentleman*, I'll say, *the incomparable Sister Angelique, on piano.* And then I'll say, *And last but not least, our fearless leader, your truly, Sister Angelique, on tenor saxophone.* I find a little showmanship goes a long way toward keeping your band and your audience engaged. Even when there's no actual band and no actual audience to engage with.

Another fun aspect of the gig is getting to nod my appreciation to the camera in response to all the cheering and applause I imagine I must be getting from the folks at home after each solo I play on each instrument. Good thing I've always had a vivid imagination.

But I do enjoy hunting for all these diverse band outfits we wear, in the local consignment shops and thrift stores, where I've found some terrific deals on vintage (well, okay—salvage) clothing. Anyway, as long as the band sounds good—or at least as good as it looks—that's what counts. In difficult times like these, you have to be creative and resourceful like there's no tomorrow. Because there very well may not be.

It all began two weeks ago, when Yin and Yang—in their physical forms—strolled into The Lowered Bar at the end of the night. I was packing up my sax as they came over to the bandstand to say hello. We greeted each other the safe way—with elbow bumps—and then they surprised me with an invitation to join them for a nightcap at their place next door.

I had run into these two out on Wickenden Street a few times before, and in the corner markets. We'd stand a safe distance apart, wearing our masks and making casual conversation about the catastrophic climate changes, the apocalyptic pandemic, the staggering death toll, the tanking economy, and so on. They were always friendly and eager to talk, and spoke to me in a way that made me think they knew me better than I knew myself. Which was weird. They called me Sister, but never mentioned their names, and, strangely, I never inquired. Judging by their odd appearance (Yin with a half-shaved head, Yang in a purple fishnet wife-beater), I figured they were probably into jazz and knew me from my gig at The Lowered Bar. Truth be told, I was milking a longtime fantasy about being recognized in public as a local jazz celebrity—the irony of which astounds me now.

The three of us were on the bandstand talking and I noticed they weren't social distancing or wearing masks this time. Fans or not, I thought, fame is no use to you if you're dead. And so, having just gotten over a minor bout with the sniffles, I decided to say something.

That was when they introduced themselves to me by name, and explained to me just who—and what—they are.

Now, I happen to be one of these *oh-yeah-prove-it-to-me* types. And so, hearing a couple of near strangers claim to be humanoid forms of the cosmic forces of Nature known as yin and yang—who supposedly possess extraordinary powers, including being impervious to harm—I have to say, my curiosity was stoked. So I doubled up my mask and thought about the relaxing nightcap that awaited, and went along with the gag.

When we got upstairs to the apartment, Yang got the key from under the doormat and unlocked the door but didn't open it. They looked at each other, and then Yin smiled at me warmly, compassionately, while Yang floated—like a ghost—right through the door. Then Yin opened it and took my hand and walked me inside and closed the door behind us and floated over to Yang and turned to me and said, Won't you come in, Sister?

Wow, I said, astonished. Nice illusion. How'd you hide the ropes and pulleys? And Yang, I said. Incredible. Straight through the door!

That's nothing, Yang said. Watch this.

Yang took two steps toward Yin and they merged their bodies together. Both were completely transparent, one juxtaposed over the other. Then Yin stepped away and suddenly they were separate and solid again.

Ta-da, Yin said. Told you. Special powers.

Speaking—I realized—was going to be a problem.

Oh, I said, moments later. This is unexpected. And totally messed up.

Yin smiled. Unexpected? In the age of pandemics? Messed up? Compared to all the darkness collecting out there?

Sister's going to bail, Yang said.

I don't think so, Yin said.

Have you guys heard about the new Variant that causes brain tumors? I said. The one where the victim hallucinates until—

Sorry, Sister, Yang said. You're not gonna be that lucky this time.

I gulped. Then I felt something snap inside. Heard it, too. Figured it had to be my mind, or what was left of it.

However, I said. It's gotta be pretty easy to pull off that sleight-of-hand stuff on someone who's been up all day and night. Running her modes and chord scales, arpeggiating her triads, transcribing Brubeck. Playing two sets at The Lowered Bar, interacting virtually with imaginary fans, signing imaginary autographs, making imaginary money. I mean, tell me it's not easy to fool somebody who…

Yin and Yang stood staring back at me, like I was the alien life form.

Okay, I said. Let's just say you've convinced me. For now. Scared me shitless, too. What's next? What's the plan? Should I be preparing to die?

Why don't you have a seat, Sister, Yang said, pointing to a raggedy old sofa partially covered with a yellowed chenille bedspread. Would you like a glass of wine? Beer?

Or something stronger, maybe? Yin said, nodding encouragingly.

I sat down. A plastic coffee table stood in front of the couch with a geranium plant sitting on top that looked dead. A dead plant—at least—made some sense. A few CDs were scattered about as well. More reality. Seeing them helped me relax a bit. One of them—being used as a coaster for a coffee mug filled with wet ashes and cigarette butts—was mine.

I'll definitely have a vodka, I said. Tito's, if you've got it. Neat. Actually, just bring the bottle, please. As soon as possible. Beer chaser.

One non-stop boilermaker coming up, Yin said. Oh, and you can lose the mask, Sister. You can't catch the Virus from us. Yang and I are insusceptible. Invulnerable. Invincible.

I watched Yin float away to get my drink and immediately felt my blood pressure spike again. I focussed my attention on the geranium, and tried to stay calm.

From all outward appearances, Yin looked female. But based on what I'd seen and heard so far, I wasn't taking anything for granted. Somewhere in her early thirties, I figured. She was beautiful, in an alien-life form kind of way. Tall and thin, with long wavy raven-black hair cascading down from the left side of her head only, shaved clean off on top and on the right. Like a punked-out Audrey Hepburn, I thought. The entire edge of the ear you could see was lined with diamond studs that sparkled like tiny floodlights. Her lips were full and black and glossy, like patent leather, and she had wide-set sky-blue eyes and a smile I imagined got her anything she wanted. She looked small on top, wearing a green and white checkered flannel shirt tucked inside tight orange leather pants that showed off an alluring figure. She chain-smoked Chesterfield Kings, lighting one off the other.

Being Yin's polar opposite, Yang was roly-poly, with a paunch, a full white beard, and what you had to assume (because of the beard) were man titties (which would've gone better on Yin). On top, he was bald and wore a red night cap that slanted down towards a small round hole in his head where his right ear should have been. Like a punked-out Santa Claus, I thought. He stood a little over doorknob height and wore cargo shorts exposing stubby hairless legs. Dark pinhole eyes went off in different directions, making it impossible to know which one to look at when you talked to him.

They both spoke with polite British accents.

I caught myself wondering what these two could possibly have been thinking of when they put together their physical profiles and picked out their wardrobes. Strange as it sounds, I could see myself helping them out with that, if we were ever to get better acquainted.

Yin reappeared suddenly and set a double shot of vodka down on the coffee table, along with a bottle of Tito's and a Narragansett Lager long-neck, and then she sat down on the sofa beside me. She lit a cigarette and placed her arm behind my neck and began fingering my Afro. Oh, she said, smiling. It's soft!

I leaned forward and reached for the vodka, grateful to be holding something familiar in my hand.

You guys, I said. When we said hello and bumped elbows a few minutes ago, I felt it. Both of you were solid. How can you be solid, I said—poking

Yin gently on the shoulder—and still pass through other solids? Including yourselves?

Funny you should mention that, Yin said. She pointed to her head. There's a switch, she said. On and off. Comes with the Special Powers kit. You download a link and install the software and—

A switch, I said.

Uh-huh, she said. She drew on her cigarette. And Sister, she said, unless you've got one of these switches, those masks you're wearing will defeat the purpose of that vodka you're drinking.

Just then, Yang plopped into the armchair next to the couch, sending a plume of dust roiling into the air. He coughed and waved his arm to dispel the particles.

We need to talk, Sister Angelique, Yang said, with one eye on me and the other aimed somewhere off in Yin's direction. We've been catching your Zoom sessions at The Lowered Bar on Tuesday nights, he said. Bought your CD, too. The one where you play all the instruments? Like Sammy Davis, Junior? Bloody cool act, Sammy's. We caught him at Cesar's in Vegas, back in the day. It's there on the coffee table under the ashtray. Your CD.

I held my head still and found it with my eyes.

Yin and I have been wondering, he said. Are you quite aware of the effect your music is having on your listeners these days?

I removed my masks and drained my drink. Effect? I said.

I'm sure you realize, he said, the world is in a very bad way.

Yes, Yin said, it's never been this bad before. Not since the beginning of time. Nature's totally pissed. And has every right to be.

Yang leaned in. We hear She's getting ready to pull the plug, he said.

I felt my jaw drop, and so I poured in a couple of fingers' worth straight from the bottle. Swallowed.

Jeez, you guys, I said. I know I'm no John Coltrane. No Sonny Rollins. No Lester Young. Maybe not even Kenny G. But I'm sure my jazz playing doesn't cause sickness and disease and death the likes of—

No, no, no, Yin said. You misunderstand, Sister. Yang and I think that you—and your magical jazz sounds—might be the only hope.

My jazz sounds? I said. Magical? I said. The only hope?

Yin looked at Yang. Her smile gone. Sister doesn't know, she said.

Sister doesn't know what? I said.

About the power of your music, Yang said. The lives it's saving.

Saving? I said. Well, I said, searching for a suitable explanation. It's what I do. I mean, you don't compliment a fish for being a good swimmer, do you? It's just what a fish does. I mean, I've been practicing a lot lately, what with the pandemic forcing everyone indoors and all. I guess my chops have improved. More so on the uptempo tunes. But how could that affect—

This isn't about chops, Yin said. It has nothing to do with chops.

It doesn't? I said.

No, silly.

Then what? I said.

Your *intentions*.

My intentions.

Look into my eyes, Yang said. Tell me what you see.

Which one? I said, getting a chuckle out of Yin.

Take your bloody pick, he said.

I stared into Yang's right eye, the one aimed more towards me.

Nothing, I said. I see nothing.

Figures, Yang said.

It's invisible to your eyes, Yin said, but not to ours.

You guys can see a person's intentions? I said. In their eyes?

Yin nodded. In their eyes, their ears, their hair, their skin, their handwriting, their—

Bowel movements, Yang chirped. Clear as the centerfold in *Playboy*, he said.

Yin extended her arm out beyond its natural length and slapped Yang on the shoulder. Yang's becoming quite the miniature perv, she said.

Your intentions are also evident in your music, Yang said. In particular, your devotion to it.

But in your case, Sister, Yin said, it's reached a level of purity that we've not seen before in a human being. Not lately, anyway. Too bad we can't bottle it. And prescribe it.

And sell it, Yang said.

Wait a minute, I said. How in the world is my devotion to jazz saving lives?

Thousands and thousands of lives, Yin said.

Oh, it's way more than that by now, Yang said.

Listeners become immune to the Virus, Yin said, after hearing two sets of your music. As played by your band. In other words, Sister—by you.

So-o-o many human lives have been saved already, Yang said, that we think you could be the one to convince the Council.

This is getting deep, I said. What Council? Convince them of what?

The members of the Gathering Of Differences, Yin said. G-O-D, she said.

Oh, that Council, I said, smacking my forehead like the knowledge had somehow slipped my mind.

You need to convince them to intercede, Yang said. And save your species from extinction.

Well, jeez, I said. I appreciate the encouragement and support and whatnot. But, you know, I'm really just a mediocre jazz player. With just the one gig, once a week, in some dump called The Lowered Bar. You've been there, you've seen it. There are much better players out there. Real pros. More established. Completely devoted. Flawless intentions. You guys could get any one of them to convince—

Exactly, Yin said. But your music is saving lives, not Kenny G's. Your solos are inoculating the masses, not Kenny G's.

And besides, Yang said, Kenny's a super busy guy. Always working the big rooms. Even during a pandemic. It's amazing. A bloody household word, he is. He'd be giving up a lot. Whereas you've got nothing to lose.

And that's why it has to be you, Yin said. There was no smile this time.

I need a minute here, guys, I said. I reached for the longneck.

Okay, Yin said. Let's give Sister some space. She grabbed Yang's hand. Come with me, shorty, she said. I'll let you fondle my kneecaps.

I'd rather lick your wrists, Yang said.

Hey, go for it, you two, I said. There's time.

Together they rose and floated through the wall and disappeared into the kitchen.

No question about it, I should've beelined it for the hills right then and there. Instead, I sipped from my beer and began recalling my days as a music major at Rhode Island Community College. During my last semester, I took an elective course in comparative religion, which is when I first learned about yin and yang. Not as humanoids with superpowers, of course, but as a philosophy. How the universe is composed of competing yet complementary forces of light and dark, sun and moon, male and female, and so on.

It was all coming back to me. How the story is over 3,500 years old, formulated in the text of the I Ching, the Chinese Book of Changes, in ninth-century BC. How the Chi-Ching—as I jokingly called it back then—is often used symbolically to provide guidance for moral decision-making, as informed by the tenets of Taoism and Confucianism and Buddhism.

I remembered how, generally speaking, the books characterized yin as inward energy, feminine in nature. Still, dark, and negative. While yang was characterized as outward energy. Masculine, hot, bright, and positive.

Hey, Sister, Yang suddenly yelled from the kitchen. Don't go believing everything you read in those bloody textbooks.

That's right, Yin hollered. Yang's not nearly as hot and bright as those books say he is.

Jeez, I said. You guys can read minds, too?

Not if you don't want us to, Yin said.

How can I trust you not to? I said.

You can't, Yang said.

Thanks for the warning, I said. I poured more vodka, and we all went back to my thoughts.

The basic idea, as I understood it, was that yin and yang elements may come in opposing or complementing pairs, but they aren't static or mutually exclusive phenomena. The world is composed of different—sometimes opposing—forces, but such forces can coexist and even complement each other. In some cases, these forces even rely on one another for their existence—the alternation of day and night, for instance, since there cannot be darkness without light.

Also, the balance struck between yin and yang energy in any given pair is important. If yin is stronger, yang will be weaker, and vice versa. And this balance is perceived to exist in everything. Even—to some degree—in yin and yang as individual forces! And to me, that was the wildest thing of all: That yin and yang can interchange under certain conditions.

So now it all came down to this: After claiming nearly a billion human lives in a few short years, the coronavirus known as COVID-19—and its multiple mutations—was raging out of control and threatening to wipe out human life on earth within the next several months. Unless the world could reach herd immunity before then. It had only gotten this bad because of the gross lack of leadership at the beginning of the pandemic by the governments of the world, coupled with society's stubbornly derelict behavior, resulting in wave upon wave of resurgences and the rise of deadly variants that made even a partial recovery impossible. And none of the vaccines could keep up.

Yin and Yang were messengers, and the message was: Nature plans to stop human beings from destroying the world, by destroying them first.

I shuddered again at the sight of Yin floating over to the couch. She touched down gracefully and topped off my glass.

I'm sure the whole flotation thing must be a blast for you guys, I said. But really, could you just keep your feet on the ground? Just while I'm around? Please?

Of course, Yin said. No problem. I'm glad to see you're getting the gist of things, Sister. What a good thing it was, taking that course in religion.

Comparative religion, I said.

Well, there's really nothing much to compare, she said. Once you boil it all down, it amounts to the same basic baloney.

No argument here, I said.

Now, she said, the Council of the Gathering Of Differences is comprised of numerous pairs of opposites, or inseparable entities. Oppos, they're called. With Life and Death being the presiding pair.

Wait, I said. Life and who?

Death, she said. Life's opposing force. Each member of each pair will take on a humanoid form, like Yang and I have, in order to interact with you on a level you can relate to. So you don't implode every two seconds, or simply die of fright.

Just then Yang floated over and landed on the coffee table with a thud.

Guys! I said. I'm already imploding every two seconds and dying of fright. Please, let's keep our feet on the ground. Okay?

You'll meet them all at the conference of Ultimate Strategies, Yang said, which will be held two weeks from tonight in the main ballroom of the Hampton Inn on Pawtucket Avenue.

You're totally making this up, I said.

Yin shook her head. Nope, we're not. You take Wickenden Street to Hope Street. Hope becomes East Avenue. Go left on Grace Street, then it's a quick right onto Pawtucket. After the first light, the Inn will be on your right.

I know where the Hampton Inn is, Yin, I said. I've played way too many lame events in that ballroom not to know.

This one won't be lame, Yang said. You'll have the time of your life, if you survive. And Sister, he said. Speaking of survival…those sniffles. Have they cleared up completely?

I think they have, I said. Wait. How do you know about my…

Yang eyed me. Really? he said.

Festivities will start promptly at 8:00 PM, Yin said, so we'll plan to get there around seven and set up the computer and the video screen and hook up the speaker system. The audio and video feeds will have to be perfect.

But why the Hampton Inn? I said. It's a stone's throw from I-95. Think of the traffic, the noise. Why not the Westin Hotel in downtown Providence? Or the Biltmore?

Yang threw up his arms. That's what I bloody said, he said. Unfortunately, Yin is dating Mr. Hampton at present. Not Mr. Westin. Nor Mr. Biltmore. And Hampie-pie wants to keep it that way.

Yin giggled.

I gazed at her. Does Hampie-pie know who you are? I said. And who else will be coming to dinner?

No way, she said. That would complicate things for everybody.

Drink up, Sister, Yang said, nodding to the beer warming in my hand. And don't worry, he said. Yin and I will be at the conference to run interference, if necessary. We'll have your back.

Yin lifted the bottle to my lips. Try and drink something, Sister, she said. You'll want to be liquored up good for this next part. She paused while I sipped.

You must make a list of all the pairs that will be in attendance at the conference, Yin said, so you can learn who's who, and chat them up during the night. You know, win their favor. Gain their confidence. Inspire their pity. Whatever you have to do.

Pour, I said. She filled my glass.

Have you got a pencil or a pen, Yang said. There'll be lots of pairs attending this year.

I reached nervously for my pockets. Yin manifested a pen out of thin air and handed it to me, along with a crumpled Dunkin Donuts bag to write on.

Ready? Yang said.

For what? I said. Selling my soul to the Devil?

Hah! Yin said. The Devil's not real, Sister. That's an old wives' tale. They made it up to scare you.

Who's they? I said.

The old wives, Yin said. As informed by the old husbands, no doubt. The early fanatics.

Yang began. Let's see, he said. Life and Death will be Masters of Ceremonies, like we said. They'll be flanking you at the head table, with Life on your left, and Death on your right. Hope and Despair will be there, too. Along with Optimism and Pessimism. Oh, and don't be confused if any two different pairs of opposites seem to overlap in some way. Certain subtleties exist that you may not be aware of.

I scoffed. Are you serious? I said. Subtleties?

War and Peace will be there for sure, Yang said. Truth and Lies are vacationing in Antigua, but no worries, Honesty and Deceit will sub for them. And we'll have other biggies in attendance this year, too, like Pleasure and Pain, Happiness and Sorrow, Feast and Famine, Good and Evil, Virtue and Sin, Plenty and Poverty. And, of course, Health and Sickness—in spite of their grueling schedule these days.

Sound and Silence will try to make an appearance, Yin said. Or so I'm told. Consonance and Dissonance will as well, with you being a jazz player.

But Sound will have nothing good to say about anything, Yang said. Especially jazz. And Silence is sure to be bored to death by everything. Win those two over, Sister, and there's a chance others may follow.

Love and Hate said they wouldn't miss it for the world, Yin said. Innocence and Guilt can't wait to meet you, also. But Guilt thinks you two've already met, which is not surprising. Guilt knows everybody from someplace.

Kindness and Cruelty may show up, Yang said. You never know about those two.

Respect and Contempt go to all these things, Yin said.

And Concern and Apathy, Yang said, the most unlikely oppos you'd ever expect to see. Raising bloody hell at a party. They'll be naked and swinging from the chandeliers after one drink.

Oppos? I said.

Short for opposites, Yin said. I already mentioned that, Sister. You must pay attention. Remember, the whole world is depending on you.

Acceptance and Rejection will be in the kitchen this year, Yang said, so I'd recommend the *Shrimp Fra Diavolo*. Always exquisite.

And Loss and Gain are doing desserts, Yin said, so be sure to specify which one you want when they take your entree order. In case they run out.

And there's sure to be the usual crowd pleasers, Yang said. Serenity and Anxiety, Arousal and Disinterest, Affection and Hostility, Anger and Humor, Contentment and Envy.

Faith and Doubt promised to stop by as well, Yin said. They'll be bringing Confidence and Skepticism. And Bravery and Fear will be Sergeants at Arms this year.

And remember the rule, Yang said. Under certain conditions, oppos can interchange freely, which may be undetectable to an untrained eye. Like yours.

Yin suddenly squealed with delight. Oh, and I received a text from Loneliness, she said. She and Companionship are working the bar again this year. So pace yourself, Sister. Especially if you're drinking tequila. The margaritas will be delicious, but poisonous. More than one and you'll likely spend the night on your ass.

Or on somebody else's ass, Yang said. And hey, he said, let's not forget. Everyone's favorite oppo of all will be here this year. Lust!

Yin blushed like a schoolgirl. Which means Aversion won't be far away.

Satisfaction and Regret never miss a conference, Yang said. And you can count on Pride and Shame to be there, too, just like in real life. The omnipresent duo.

Trust and Suspicion will manage the cloakroom, Yin said. Self and Other, Loyalty and Betrayal, Order and Chaos have all RSVP'd in the affirmative, as well.

Last and quite least, Yang said, Compassion and Indifference will be waiting tables. And do not tip them, no matter how much they complain.

The conference will attract scores of oppos, Yin said. But don't worry, Sister. They will all be wearing name tags in case you forget who's who. Although some will remove them. Or worse, switch them up for the fun of it.

Regardless, Yang said. They'll all know who you are. Even if, at some point during the night, you no longer do.

Name tags? I said, dizzy with disbelief. I'd still like a word with the Devil, if you can arrange it.

The debate will begin at midnight, Yin said. Each oppo will have an opportunity to throw in his or her two cents' worth. As soon as the debate concludes, the voting will start. Each member of each pair gets to cast one ballot, in favor of salvation or damnation. In the case of a tie, Yang and I will draw straws to see which one of us gets to break it.

And humanity better hope it's Yin, Yang said.

The goal, Yin said, is for you to use your music in an intentional act of love to inoculate enough human beings before Conference day to convince a majority of the members that human kind deserves another chance. If you succeed, Nature will abide by the Council's decision and allow a recovery from the pandemic. However, this will be the last chance your species gets to do things right. There won't be another.

You have two weeks, Yang said.

Got it, I said. No problem. Piece a cake. I'll have to cancel a dentist appointment, but...they're good about rescheduling.

Yin smiled again, sadly this time. You should know, Sister, that the Council has never before been persuaded to intercede on humanity's behalf. Not by anyone. Not Buddha. Not Christ. Not Mohammed.

Not even by Mohammed Ali, Yang said. We hung them all out to dry. Left them all on their own. Of course, they each had some minor successes on their own, but things were never as—

Bad as they are now? I said. I can relate. Life's a bitch.

That may well be, Yin said. But I wouldn't dare say it out loud, Sister— or even think it—at the conference. And never to her face.

Yang hung his head. Change comes hard to this crowd, Sister. Like moving a cemetery hard.

So start blowing that horn, Yin said. And burn that beat of yours, Sister Angelique.

You'll have to rock out round the clock, Yang said, to keep all those bloody heads from exploding.

The rest of the night was as sleepless as they come. Lying in bed in my flat, I thought about escaping. But then, ever try to *not* think of a good place to hide so the mind readers can't find you—and then go hide there? My mind felt toasted to a crisp, but I couldn't stop thinking. Humanoids? Jazz fans? Of mine? My music saving lives? Kenny G—a bloody household word? These and other disturbing thoughts kept haunting me.

I tried to meditate, to barricade myself in the present moment. I'd have settled for any moment in the past, too. But all I could do was imagine myself two weeks from now, mingling with Yin and Yang and the Council of the Gathering Of Differences at the Conference of Ultimate Strategies in the ballroom of the Hampton Inn on Pawtucket Avenue, where I would be in charge of saving the world.

I hate to whine, but nothing in life prepares you for such a thing.

At 6:02 AM the phone rang. It was Yin. She said to bring all my instruments and computer equipment to The Lowered Bar right away, and we'd start making more backing tracks and playing the Zoom videos of my previous gigs for the world to hear. The idea being to create a super-spreader event for the "cure" this time, instead of the disease.

I spent every day and night for the next week recording new material and performing continuous jazz sets at the club, which were broadcast live. I wrote new tunes for the band, composed my own original jazz melodies on the chords of some well-known pop songs, re-arranged a handful of jazz standards, even jazzed up a Kenny G tune (at Yang's insistence), and basically blew my brains out from dawn to dawn. Also, the band had to sightread all this new material on the gig, since there was no time to rehearse it. Fortunately, I *am* the band, so it wasn't a big deal.

Then, at the beginning of the second week, Yin and Yang came to me and said we needed to talk.

What's up, guys, I said. Everything okay?

Hold still, Sister, Yin said, wrapping her hands around the sides of my neck. Your glands are swollen. I don't like how it stings when you swallow.

I eyed her. How did you know… Never mind, I said. Of course my glands are swollen. Of course it stings to swallow. I've been blowing into a saxophone for a solid week. You have to expect some wear and tear.

Then I coughed.

She held out her hand and manifested a glass and handed it to me. Gargle with this, she said. Salt and water. Three times a day till it's better. We can't afford to screw things up now.

Yeah, okay, I said. Like I don't have enough going on and you want me to gargle three times a day.

Plus, you've been coughing in your sleep, Yang said. Not a good sign. And that dream you had on Saturday night. The long, hot, wet one. What was that all about? You still feeling anxious? Horny?

For Christ's sake, Yang, I said. Stay out of my frigging dreams.

Yin took my arm in hers and pulled me aside. Now, Sister, she said. This is your destiny. This act of love you're performing will be remembered as humanity's crowning achievement. No other human being has ever—

More like an act of fear, I said. Then I coughed again. It might help, you know, if you laid off the smokes, I said. Secondhand smoke is no joke. As you undoubtedly know, Yin. I eyed her. Like you know everything else that happens to me.

Yin blanched. I swear to you, Sister, she said. Crashing your dream was Yang's idea. I hid my eyes in my hands the whole time we were there. Out of respect.

Aw, gee, I said. How noble. What about your ears? Did you block them up, too?

Well, Yin said. I only have two hands.

By the day of the conference, an estimated one hundred million people had been inoculated worldwide through exposure to my jazz videos, and were now immune to the Virus. Also, I was finally getting known as a jazz player. (So Yang, you want to talk who's playing the big rooms now? How's a hundred mil sound? Big enough for you? You and your buddy Kenny? Figures.)

At 7:00 on the night of the conference, Yin and Yang and I arrived at the Hampton Inn in Pawtucket. I'd decided on a lilac zoot suit, with a low-cut pink chiffon blouse and choker, earning wild hoots of approval from Yin and sexy whistles from Yang. We hooked up my computer to a large video screen and two audio speakers and set everything up on the stage. At 8:00 the members of the Council of the Gathering Of Differences began manifesting in the lobby in their humanoid forms, and making their way to the ballroom.

I had invited a handful of friends for moral support, all of whom had been vetted by Yin and Yang. My mentor and former sax teacher, Fontaine Vitale, was there, with his vintage Selmer Mark VI tenor saxophone in hand, for when the event turned into a jam session. He brought his bass player, the magnificent Slam Pizzicato. These two local jazz legends had become world famous after appearing as minor characters in an acclaimed novel of 2019 called, *A Brief Madness: New Identity*—a nail-biting psychological thriller set in the mean streets of South Providence, penned by a former jazzman whose name I can't recall at the moment. But you can find the title in paperback and e-book on Amazon.

Other friends in attendance were Albright K. Westinghouse, a hip jazz piano player I've worked countless gigs with over the years, and his therapist, a psycho-jazz-guitar-apist named Jerome Weisberg, owner of the Ponderosa East Jazz Club in Cranston. Two other dear friends from

South County were there as well, named Joys and Hel O'Rock, and their big-brained cat, John. Also, the virtuosic jazz trombonist Blue Carson (formerly with the Cootie Verman Big Band) and his partner, a hottie named Louise; and the brilliant young writer Clifford Seeks, who brought along some dipshit named Ziggy Zigarelli. Retired race relations counselor Sal Withers and his girlfriend Amy Dunn and their dog Francis were there (Go, Team Francis!). And finally, Janis Scott Joplin, a transgender news reporter for the *Choctaw Sun Advocate* down in Butler, Alabama, whose reviews of my Zoom jazz videos had gone viral on social media, and who had agreed to document the conference for posterity.

The event began promptly at 8:00 as scheduled, with drinks, hors d'oeuvres and dancing—music courtesy of canned performances by none other than the Sister Angelique Victoria Etwombe Jazz Quartet. Now, I've seen plenty of professional drinkers in my time—even qualified as one myself, back in the day—but I never saw the sauce being tossed back the way these humanoids sucked it down. Another one of their special powers, I guess.

At 9:00 we all found our seats at banquet tables beautifully decorated with extravagant floral arrangements. Each circular table sat twelve humanoids—or six pairs of oppos. I located my name card at the middle of the rectangular head table that faced out into the room. Directly in front of my place setting sat the dead geranium from Yin and Yang's apartment. Just in case.

As Yin and Yang had forewarned, I was flanked at my seat by Life and Death—the two presiding oppos—with Life on my left, and Death on my right. In a bizarre twist—but then, what twist wouldn't have been?—they had decided to attend the conference as twins. Identical. And androgynous.

To top it off, they came dressed as Royal Canadian Mounted Police, but without the mounts (or, as they insisted, *Gendarmerie Royale du Canada*). I must admit, I was impressed by their outfit, and had visions of adapting it for the bandstand: A red serge tunic with gold buttons, solid blue collars and blue pointed-sleeve cuffs; black leather cylindrical forearm guards and riding gloves; dark blue breeches with yellow-gold strapping tucked into over-the-calf brown leather riding boots; a carrying pouch set on a cross-belt with a sidearm holstered high on the hip; and a beige broad-brimmed felt hat, with a high crown, pinched symmetrically at the four corners.

Cops never looked so hot, I thought.

But the truly bad news came when they entered the ballroom and refused to wear their name tags.

Yin immediately sidled over to me and told me once again not to worry. That she and Yang could easily tell the difference between Life and Death, and would be there to help, if I was ever in doubt.

Ever in doubt? I said. Me?

She smirked, then had the chutzpah to ask me who my partner was in my dream.

Well, Yin, I said. You were there. You should've peeked when you had the chance.

Actually, Sister, I did. But neither Yang nor I recognized him. Only that he—

Unbelievable, I said.

Yes, Yin said, smiling. He certainly was.

No! I said. You guys.

Oh, come on, Sister, she said. You can tell me. I promise I won't—

Get your own lovers, Yin, I said. This one—whoever he was—is mine.

As soon as Life and Death sat down, and before any formal introductions had been made, the one sitting to my right—Death, supposedly—leaned over and whispered in my ear.

Say, Sister, he said. *Is it true you're a nun? Or a wannabe?*

What? I said. No way. You mean you didn't already know that?

Just making sure, he said. *So*, he said, *these two hillbillies were talking one day, and one of them says to the other, Hey Jeb, if I was to disguise myself and sneak into your house and have relations with your wife, would that make us kin? And the other one says, No. It'd make us even.*

Death sat there looking at me—brows raised, mouth open wide, eyes full of mischief—like he'd just delivered the line of the century.

A half-hearted smile was the best I could do. Humor-wise, the old oppo had just lived up to his name.

You must be Death, I said.

He nodded.

But how do I know that for sure? I said. Other than from that joke.

Death shrugged. *You'll never know for sure*, he said, *unless I show you.*

Show me? I said. You mean, as in make something die?

As in make someone *die*, he said. He smiled devilishly. *Wanna see?*

No! I said. Forget it. I'm fine, I'm fine.

Well, he said, winking. *I can see that.*

Oh my god, I thought, Death is flirting with me. I swallowed hard. You like jokes? I said.

The funny ones, yeah, he said.

Stop me if you've heard this one, I said. Jesus is sitting on a park bench feeding the birds and Billy spots him and runs over and says, Hey, aren't you Jesus? And Jesus says, Yes, Billy, I am. And Billy says, How did you know my name? And Jesus says, Because I'm Jesus. Oh, Billy says. So Jesus, he says, I've heard you listen to prayers. Do you listen to prayers? And Jesus says, No, Billy, I don't listen to prayers. I listen to jazz.

Hah! Death said. *Cute. I see you're into religion.*

I am not into religion, I said. That was your takeaway? From my joke?

Here's one you'll really like, then, he said. *Father Murphy's visiting the Sunday school class, and—*

Wait, I said. You know Father Murphy? From Wickenden Street Manor?

Doesn't everybody? Death said. *By now?*

Tell you what, Death, I said. I'll stick to the sax, you stick to the Virus.

I prefer the Variant, Death said. *You know, the new one that gives you brain tumors. And then you hallucinate till your head explo—*

Whatever, I said. Let's just agree to leave the jokes to the pros. Okay?

Deal, Death said. He sipped from his water glass. *Guess what?* he said. *I was there. On the front lines.*

Front lines? I said.

At the Battle of Modern Jazz, Death said.

There was a battle? I said.

Are you kidding? he said. *I won it for you. Singlehandedly.*

You? I said. Won the Battle of Modern Jazz? For me?

Yup. For all of us.

How did you win it? I said, incredulous. Do you play?

Death nodded. *Drums*, he said. *It was brutal out there. Good players were dropping like flies. So I threatened to wipe out smooth jazz entirely. Destroy all those bogus honey-coated wimpy-ass pseudo-bluesy cliché pentatonic licks once and for all, and rid the world of all those digitally programmed rhythm section tracks as well—all that sad sampled shit—and that brought the bastards to their knees. They couldn't wait to sign the armistice. Soon you'll be hearing modern jazz in elevators, dentist offices, hardware stores, beauty salons. Even Congress. Sun Ra is on McConnell's playlist.*

Sorry, Death, I said. I'll have to hear that to believe it.

Death eyed me suspiciously. *And where were you hiding out,* he said, *while the battle was raging? In your practice room, I'll bet. Running your silly modes and chord scales, probably. Arpeggiating your triads. Transcribing Brubeck. While I was out defending the a-rhythmic perimeter of atonal harmony and melodic chaos!*

Death had struck a nerve. I was not going to sit there and take that kind of talk from anyone.

What's wrong with practicing my modes and chord scales? I said. And arpeggiating my triads? And for your information, Brubeck's jazz playing isn't half as bad as it sounds. Have you ever tried to play jazz? I said. For a living? In the real world? Instead of just standing around and defending it? We professionals don't spend all our time on the bandstand, you know. There's tons of preparation that goes into it. Serious effort. Years and years' worth, that the public never hears about. And we players never get paid for.

That's a crock, Death said. *Jazz is in your ear. And your heart and your soul. Not your head. Period. Case closed.*

And how the heck would you know that? I railed.

Oh Sister, Life said, coming to my rescue. *Don't mind Death. He's just venting.*

Death stood up and scoffed and stormed off. I turned to my left.

So, I said, you're Life?

Isn't it obvious? Life said.

Jeez, I said. Even your voices sound exactly alike. Did you guys have to practice that? I said. You and Death?

Death doesn't practice, Life said. *He figures what's the point? You can't win against him. Everything dies, eventually. And he is Death, after all.*

How do you put up with him? I said. He acts like a spoiled child.

173

I know, Life said. *He's used to getting his way. And now he's really feeling his oats, scoring big with this pandemic. Figures he's on a roll, especially with this new variant. It's his way or the highway. What can an oppo do?*

Well, I said, there's Prozac. Psilocybin. Magic mushrooms. Ayahuasca. Medical marijuana. Bloody Marys. Acupuncture. Chiropractic. Timeouts. Talk therapy. Mormonism.

We've tried it all, Life said. *We've had the best shaman in the rainforest out hunting for his spirit animal, but… It's kind of late in the game for drugs and religion. And no therapists will take him. So he gets mad, and takes them.*

Death takes his therapists? I said. For not treating him?

Not directly, Life said. *He doesn't like getting his hands dirty. He'll have something or someone else do it for him. You know, like cancer. Big Macs. Trump supporters. Trump. Don Junior. Jared. Ivanka. Rudy…*

What about Pence? I said. You didn't mention Pence.

Pence is on the fence, she said. *Poor guy's still really scared. And confused.*

Why am I not surprised? I said.

I know, Life said. *Tough choices. Such is life.*

Easy for you to say, I said.

Life smiled. *Thanks for not calling me a bitch, by the way. Many do.*

Not to your face, I wouldn't think, I said, nervously. Remembering.

Life eyed me. *Not the smart ones.*

I nodded. Relieved. So, I said, what would make *your* life better?

Oh, I don't need much, Life said. *A little appreciation on a daily basis would be nice, I suppose. A lot more live-and-let-live from you people.*

No argument here, I said. I sighed. Love your outfit, by the way.

I know you do, Life said. She winked. *And I agree, a few touch ups here and there, and it'll look terrific on the bandstand.*

Prosciutto di Parma con meloni and an antipasti loaded with sweet peppers and onions and olives and anchovies and real Parmigiano-Reggiano cheese got everyone's mouth watering and appetite surging. For the second plate, I went with Yang's recommendation, the *Shrimp Fra Diavolo* (literally, Brother Devil—the popular name given to Michele Pezza, a famous guerrilla leader who resisted the French occupation of Naples during the late 1700s, who also happened to be an old boyfriend of Yin's). A tad spicy, but fabulous. And for dessert, they offered a choice of Tiramisu or zeppoles, dusted with powdered sugar and crowned with a syrupy Italian cherry. I went with both. Dutifully.

Then, after polishing off my third margarita—blessed by Don Julio Anejo, the Cadillac of tequilas—I got out my sax and waddled on stage and started to blow. Solo style. Free as a bird. With no chord changes from some old song to fence me in or hold me back. Just Sister Angelique and her magical jazz sounds, serenading a world of opposites in the age of COVID.

Before I knew it, Fontaine had grabbed his sax, Slam his bass, Blue his trombone, Dr. Weisberg his guitar, and Albright had found the piano, and then—with Death himself sitting in on drums—we jammed on a tune by Wayne Shorter called "Armageddon". An appropriate number, I thought. Considering.

Love was filling that ballroom to the brim through the music, and the requests started pouring in. First we covered the standard jazz repertoire, including favorites like Lil Armstrong's "Struttin' With Some Barbecue", Duke Ellington's "Take The A Train", Thelonious Monk's "Round Midnight", Charlie Parker's "Boplicity", Dizzy Gillespie's "Salt Peanuts", Sonny Rollins's "Saint Thomas", Nat Adderley's "Work Song", and Joe Zawinul's "Birdland". We even threw in Dave Brubeck's "Take Five" (as borrowed from Paul Desmond) for good measure. Although Death could not keep the meter locked in 5/4 time on the drums, and so he had to play free over the form. The wimp.

Then we ventured into more obscure fare, like Charles Mingus's "Reincarnation Of A Lovebird", and John Coltrane's "A Love Supreme", and Miles Davis's "Miles Runs the Voodoo Down", from *Bitches Brew*.

We rocked out for a good two hours, with no breaks. And for our final tune, we honored Death's request for Ornette Coleman's "Song X", and blew the roof off the place. The crowd went nuts. These humanoids loved their jazz hot *and* cool, loud *and* soft, fast *and* slow, swingin' high *and* swingin' low— just as you'd expect from a bunch of wild and crazy booze-soaked oppos.

At midnight everyone returned reluctantly to their seats, while the other players in the band remained on stage with me. I'd gotten so lost in the music that, for a time, I had forgotten why we were there. One of the things about playing is that it can interrupt your thoughts and hold you in the present moment. You vanish into the sound of each note, each beat, each instrument, the infinite present—where the music happens—and you get a little respite from your little life. Your mind becomes silent and still, a vast, empty, trouble-free place. A place where even the mind readers can't find you, because there's no mind there for them to read. No you to be found.

But then, of course, the debate began, and the world snapped back into shape. Reflexively. And again, I saw myself standing there. Small. Finite. And found.

There was little said on either side of the argument. It seemed everyone's mind was already made up, and from the discussions I'd had with various members of the Council throughout the night, it was going to be close.

Half an hour later, they voted.

As the ballots were being tallied, I noticed a headache forming behind my eyes. It quickly grew worse, and I started to sweat. Suddenly I felt feverish. My hands went numb. I felt nauseous. The band was looking at me. Sister? I heard someone say. Are you all right?

Must be nerves, I thought. I looked out at the packed and now silent ballroom. What was once a lively party had turned solemn and somber.

Damn.

As they headed for the mic to announce the verdict, I heard my horn hit the floor.

Then my eyes closed, and my knees buckled, and I landed beside it.

Someone must have thrown water in my face to revive me, because I was all wet when I came to. I was still lying on the floor at center stage, the Council standing in a circle around me. Some of them muttering to themselves, some snickering, some looking worried, some filming the scene on their phones, some talking on them and ignoring everything.

Yin was sitting on the floor—smoking—with my head in her lap. Yang was standing beside her.

Hi Sister, Yin said, holding up the geranium. Feeling better?

Life and Death—the Royal Mounted Androgynous Twins—were once again flanking me, with one of them kneeling at my right, and the other at my left. Still no name tags.

The room was spinning slowly. I felt limp.

Feel her hair, Yin said, puffing away.

The Gendarme on my right reached over and squeezed my Afro. *Oh, he or she said. It's soft.*

Then the one on my left took hold of my hand. *Good job, tonight, Sister,* he or she said. *Humanity will be talking about this for a while.*

About what? I said.

Unless they screw up again, the one on my right said, still fingering my hair. *Which they will.*

But you don't know that for sure, I mumbled. Or do you?

Well, the other one said, *we think it might be best if you come with us, Sister. GOD can use a hot player like you. You can lead the band.*

I don't like the sound of that, I said. What's God got to do with this?

Not God, he or she said. *The Gathering Of Differences. G-O-D.*

Am I dying? I said. Do I have the Virus? That frigging Variant? The one that gives you brain tumors and then—

Look over here, the one on my right said. *How many Bengal tigers am I holding in my hand?*

I looked closely. Two, I said.

Four, he or she said. *Yeah, you're dying.*

But I can't be dying, I said. My music saves lives. That must mean mine, too, right?

Good question, the one on my left said. *Has anyone checked on that?*

It doesn't make sense, I said. Maybe I ate something. Feels like food poisoning. Head-to-toe style.

I think you're dying, Yang said.

But if my jazz playing makes people immune by hearing it, then it must make me immune, too. I mean, I'm human. I hear it. It's my damn music.

Well, the one on my right said, *it's like I always say when it comes to these situations: Absence of evidence is not evidence of absence.*

Oh come on, I said. Stop ripping off Carl Sagan.

Who do you think gave Carl that line?

This can't be happening, I said. I can't be dying. After all the work I—

All we know, Sister, the one on the left said, *is that you played your butt off on that bandstand tonight. You may have the Variant, you may be seeing and hearing things, you may be dying…but…you wowed that crowd tonight. From the moment you started blowing your horn till the moment you stopped.*

I did? I said.

Yes, you certainly did, the one on my right said. *And how is that even possible? By a mere human being? And a female jazzman to boot?*

I already told you, I said. Practice! There's as much art in practicing jazz as there is in performing it. Performing is just practicing with other people in the room. Hopefully. A few at least. It's all just practice for the next time.

Jeez, Sister, someone said. *Don't get all zen on us.*

My head was throbbing. I was shivering and burning up at the same time. Maybe it was the shrimp, I said. A couple of them tasted funny to me.

I mean, what do I know, the one on my right said. *I'm just a Gendarme Royale du Canada. But those other musicians? They know. And they were blown away.*

By the way, Sister, Yang said. I had the shrimp. And I feel fine.

You're a frigging cosmic force of Nature! I cried. Impervious to harm. Of course you feel fine.

Yin giggled. Here, Sister. Would you like to hold your plant?

I was talking to Sickness and Health, I said. Before dinner. Sickness looked pretty darn sick to me. Maybe I caught something from her.

Sickness always has one foot in the grave, the one on my left said. *But you had Sound and Silence mesmerized, Sister. First time ever—if memory serves—Sound had absolutely nothing negative to say.*

Could've been the prosciutto, I said. Anyone else eat the prosciutto?

We all ate the prosciutto, Yang said. And we all feel fine. Except you.

And Silence? the one on my left said. *She can't shut up about you. She's at the bar right now, with Consonance and Dissonance. The three of them blah blahing away about how well you blew your trumpet all night long.*

It's a saxophone! I said. Okay, time to call a doctor. Where's Health? What about Health?

And…more importantly…you saved lives, the one on my left said.

Whose lives? I said, fading fast. Everyone's but mine, apparently.

Don't go getting your hopes up, Sister, the one on my right said. *Health is not an actual MD.*

Are you saying this is the Variant? I said. That I'm dreaming this whole thing up?

That was a true act of love coming off that bandstand tonight, Sister, the one on my left said. *That was no dream.*

Enough! I cried. Which one of you is Death? I said. And I want the truth. No more shenanigans.

They looked at each other, then at me. I was soaked in sweat. My nose was dripping. My eyes were tearing. My teeth were itching. My headache had a headache. Rodents were mating inside my stomach.

I am, said the one to my right.

I turned my head and squinted. Show me those drum sticks then, I said.

Death reached a hand behind his back and took them out and held them up.

You should be ashamed of yourself, I said. You need to practice your damn tempos. You're always rushing the beat, or slowing it way the hell down. You've got no chops at all in 5/4 meter. You were totally useless on Brubeck's "Take Five". Or is it Desmond's?

I was? Death said. *I don't? I am? I do? I should?*

Damn right you were, I said. You don't. You are. You do. You should. And those drum fills? I said. They. Go. Nowhere. And connect to nothing. You can't do that on the bandstand, I said. It ruins everything. Good players will never want to play with you.

Shit, Death said. *I'm sorry, Sister. What an asshole. I had no idea.*

Yeah well, there's Prozac, I said. Psilocybin. Magic mushrooms.

I'll start practicing, Death said. *I promise. You can be my teacher. Looks like we'll be spending a lot more time together from now on.*

You're going to start practicing? I said. Why? Everything dies.

Why not, Sister? I have the time. Literally, if not musically.

Maybe it was the pastry, I said. The Tiramisu. The zeppole.

Ah-ha, Yang said. And you went with both. Figures.

Nothing about anything happening here *figures,* Yang, I said.

I was losing energy. I could feel my body getting lighter, thinner, less substantial. Morphing into something else. But there was one more thing I had to know.

Death? I said.

Yes, Sister, Death said.

That joke I told you today, I said. Had you ever heard it before I told it to you?

No, Death said.

But you knew the punch line before I got to it, didn't you? I could tell.

Eh…yes, Death said.

Well then, I said, what's the point?

To what? Death said.

To anything! I said. Everything. If you already know the answer.

Why are you asking me? Death said. *I mean, maybe there's no point.*

Oh brother, I said. Here we go. No point to any of it?

Well, if I had to guess, Death said, *I'd say the point is…to keep things balanced.*

That's it? I said. Balance?

Sure, Death said. *There's Life and there's Death. There's Everything and there's Nothing. There're all these oppos hanging around. Each one needs the other, right? To exist? So. Somebody's got to be there. Paying attention. Keeping things balanced. Which means—dead or alive—you always have a place to go, a place to be. Something to do. In one form or another. It might not be what you want it to be. Or expect it to be. But. It's comforting, isn't it? To know that you're needed? And that's the point.*

Just then my mind did a perfect backflip and went blank. I could see Yin's cigarette smoke swirling overhead, the dead geranium in her hand. Yang waving at me, mouthing goodbye. I could feel the pain coursing through my body, but I had no thoughts about the content of my experience. It was like I was observing my suffering from a great distance away. There was only the quiet, calm sense that everything was fine. That death—if it came—would be okay. Not a bad thing. Transitional. Hopefully. Well earned, even.

A restful equanimity came over me. I turned my head to the right.

Death, I said. What if I was to disguise myself and sneak into your dreams and have relations with you? Would that make us kin?

Sister! Yin cried. You cannot say such things to Death.

Death laughed. *No, Sister,* he said, eyes full of mischief. *It would make us even.*

READ HAL CROOK'S DEBUT NOVEL

A Brief Madness: New Identity is a high-voltage psychological thriller that shines the light on social and racial injustice, vigilante violence, sexual assault, human trafficking, and—more philosophically—the illusory nature of the self and how it impacts our attitudes toward good and evil.

The time is the recent global recession, when government cutbacks have squeezed law enforcement's power to protect and serve, and one family pays the price for it in blood. The setting encompasses the mean streets of South Providence, Rhode Island, the pristine coast and backwoods of Little Rhody's South County, and the smallest state's largest landfill.

A Brief Madness: New Identity shares elements with such best-sellers as *The Silence of the Lamb*s by Thomas Harris (brilliant female protagonist pursues serial killer), *Death Wish* by Brian Garfield (vigilante justice), and *A Time to Kill* by John Grisham (racial bias, revenge); but it also fills a unique niche by questioning the assumption that higher consciousness and criminality are mutually exclusive.

HAL CROOK

Hal Crook is a professor emeritus, Berklee College of Music, Boston, and an internationally known jazz musician, composer, arranger, and teacher. He has published four books on jazz improvisation, and one novel, *A Brief Madness: New Identity*, available on amazon.com and through booksellers everywhere.

Inspired by the writing of poets Donald Hall, Mary Oliver, Esperanza Spalding, and I. Michael Grossman, Crook is currently at work on a collection of poems entitled *Unsolicited: Non-Essential Writings from the Head and Heart*.

Crook lives in Rhode Island with his wife Joyce and two feral cats—John and Sharon—of "Big Brains in Our Midst" fame.

Windborne Tales: Seven Stories is his first collection of tales.

www.halcrook.com

Your reaction to this book is important.
Please offer your thoughts and leave a review on Amazon.

Made in the USA
Middletown, DE
23 December 2022

16756577R00110